Welcome ...

Mills & Boon® ... ...
you back to th... ...
nestled on... ...
With sandy beaches and breathtaking landscapes
Penhally is a warm, bustling community,
cared for by the Penhally Bay Surgery team,
led by the distinguished and
commanding Dr Nick Tremayne.

We're bringing you four new books set in
this idyllic coastal town, where fishing boats
bob up and down in the bay, friendly faces line
the cobbled streets and romance flutters on
the Cornish sea breeze! We've got gorgeous
Mediterranean heroes, top-notch city surgeons,
and the return of Penhally's very own
bad-boy rebel! But that's not all...

We step back into the life of enigmatic,
guarded hero Dr Nick Tremayne, and
nurse Kate Althorpe—the one woman who
has stolen Nick's heart and the only woman
he won't allow himself to love! Dr Nick's
unquestionable professional skill and dedication
to the Penhally Bay Surgery hide his private
pain—his is a story that will pierce your heart.

So turn the page and meet them for yourself...

**And if you've never visited Penhally before,
step right in and enjoy Medical™ Romance's
most popular miniseries. There is a
world of romantic treats awaiting you.**

Dear Reader

When I was asked to kick off the latest round of Penhally stories I was delighted—not least because it meant working again with two of my favourite authors, Kate Hardy and Margaret McDonagh, and 'meeting' Anne Fraser, who is relatively new to Medical™ Romance. We all worked together really closely on this little collection, because not only were there the interlinking stories in these four books, but also the whole existing infrastructure of Penhally Bay and St Piran, which had over the last year or so become entirely real to those of us involved. It was a chance to revisit old friends, to bring in new ones and to spend more time (sadly only in my head!) in a place I've grown to love.

It's been a pleasure and a privilege to work with people I've come to call friends, and a chance to write a really involving and emotionally challenging story. Both Sam and Gemma have suffered life-changing challenges. One drove them apart; the other has brought them back together. But can they really forgive and forget? This is the story of their journey, and I hope you get as much pleasure from reading it as I had writing it. I give it to you with my love and best wishes.

If you're revisiting Penhally, welcome back, and if this is your first trip, I hope you'll love being here as much as I do.

Caroline

THE REBEL OF PENHALLY BAY

BY
CAROLINE ANDERSON

™ MILLS & BOON®

For Clare, who has walked this road, for Dan and the children, who've held her hand along the way, and for the countless others who walk it with her. Safe journey.

First published in Great Britain 2009
Harlequin Mills & Boon Limited,
Eton House, 18-24 Paradise Road, Richmond, Surrey TW9 1SR

© Caroline Anderson 2009

ISBN: 978 0 263 86873 9

Set in Times Roman 10½ on 12¼ pt
03-1009-49458

Printed and bound in Spain
by Litografia Rosés, S.A., Barcelona

Caroline Anderson has the mind of a butterfly. She's been a nurse, a secretary, a teacher, run her own soft-furnishing business, and now she's settled on writing. She says, 'I was looking for that elusive something. I finally realised it was variety, and now I have it in abundance. Every book brings new horizons and new friends, and in between books I have learned to be a juggler. My teacher husband John and I have two beautiful and talented daughters, Sarah and Hannah, umpteen pets, and several acres of Suffolk that nature tries to reclaim every time we turn our backs!' Caroline also writes for the Mills & Boon® Romance series.

Recent titles by the same author:

Medical™ Romance

THE VALTIERI MARRIAGE DEAL
A MUMMY FOR CHRISTMAS
THEIR MIRACLE BABY*
CHRISTMAS EVE BABY*

Mills & Boon® Romance

TWO LITTLE MIRACLES
THE SINGLE MUM AND THE TYCOON
HIS PREGNANT HOUSEKEEPER

Brides of Penhally Bay

BRIDES OF PENHALLY BAY

Bachelor doctors become husbands and fathers—
in a place where hearts are made whole.

**Look out for these four books
set in the picturesque town of Penhally,
nestled on the rugged Cornish coast.**

**This month we're back in Penhally
as bad-boy doc Sam Cavendish tries to win back
his long-lost wife...**
The Rebel of Penhally Bay by Caroline Anderson

**Next month midwife Annie meets gorgeous
Spanish doctor Dr Raphael Castillo,
and one magical night leads to one little miracle...**
Spanish Doctor, Pregnant Midwife by Anne Fraser

**In December there's a real treat in store as gorgeous
high-flying heart surgeon James arrives in Penhally!**
Falling for the Playboy Millionaire by Kate Hardy

**And in January there's a new GP in town when
Italian doctor and single father Luca d'Azzaro
brings his twin babies to Penhally**
A Mother for the Italian's Twins by Margaret McDonagh

PROLOGUE

HE WASN'T concentrating.

If he'd been concentrating, he might have seen it, but he wasn't. He was miles away, in Cornwall, thanks to his mother and the letter he'd just been handed on his way out of the hospital.

It was all the usual blah.

> Hope you're well, Jamie's done well in his exams, goodness knows how, he's so idle, who does that remind you of? Oh, well, if he turns out as well as you he'll be all right but why you want to bury yourself in Africa, goodness knows. I wish you were here, you could keep him in order...

Fat chance of that. They were like peas in a pod, and the only thing that would keep Jamie in order was Jamie, as Sam very well knew.

But then the letter changed.

> I've seen Gemma again, by the way, and she asked after you. I can't believe it's ten years since you had that fling with her. You've hardly been back

since, but maybe you'll come now, with her here. Bit of an incentive for you—more interesting than your boring old mother. She's a brilliant practice nurse, and still single, though I can't imagine why when she's so gorgeous, but there doesn't seem to be anyone else around for her and she seemed very keen to hear all about you. You missed a chance there, Sam. Maybe you should come home and take up where you left off...

He hadn't read the rest. He'd screwed it up, hurled it into the bin and stalked out into the sun. Damn. He'd meant to leave before dawn, but what with one thing and another, and now the bloody letter...

The bike was loaded, stocked up for the run to the makeshift little clinic thirty miles away, and he had enough to do without distractions. He really—*really*!—didn't need to be thinking about Gemma, or that summer all those years ago. Ten, for God's sake. A whole decade. Ten long, lonely years. And he hadn't *missed* his chance, he'd had it snatched away from him—

'Oh, dammit to hell.'

He kicked the starter viciously, dropped the bike forwards off the stand and straddled it while he fastened his helmet. Why the *hell* was she back in Penhally? And why, more to the point, was she working as a practice *nurse*? So much for her dedication to medicine—but that was just par for the course, really, wasn't it? After all, she hadn't stuck to him, either.

He twisted the throttle, listened to the feeble sound of the little engine and mourned his old bike. Gemma had loved his bike, and they'd gone everywhere on it. They'd been inseparable for a year, every time she'd come down from Bath with her parents to their holiday cottage, and they'd had so much fun.

Not that her parents had approved of him, but, then, they wouldn't, would they? Not with his bad-boy reputation, and they'd had to do a fair amount of sneaking around to be together. But that second summer she'd come down alone after her final school exams, for the last summer before uni, and instead of it being the end, in a way it was to be the beginning—the beginning of the next phase of their lives. They'd got places at the same medical school in Bristol, and everything was panning out perfectly.

So he'd asked her to marry him and crazily, unbelievably, she'd said yes, so on a glorious day in early August they'd made their vows—vows he'd really meant, vows from the heart—and they'd honeymooned in the tumbledown little wooden shack on the beach that was his home for the summer, a retreat from the demands of home, a haven of tranquillity at first and then, with Gemma, a place of paradise—until her parents had come down from Bath and found them there.

They'd gone crazy, and Gemma had been in floods of tears, but she'd stood her ground, told them they were married and he'd shut the door in their faces and held her while she cried.

And then just days later, she'd left a note to say she'd changed her mind about them, and about going to uni. She wasn't sure if she wanted to read medicine after all, and she was deferring for a year and taking time out to think about things, going travelling—Gemma, who'd already seen the world with her wealthy parents—and going alone. She didn't want to see him again. And she was gone, she and her parents who'd obviously meant more to her than he had, their holiday home empty, closed up for the winter.

He'd never seen her again. Not a word, in all these years, all the time he'd been at med school in Bristol, keeping an eye on his family from a close distance and waiting and hoping for her to change her mind—he'd even been to see her parents, but they'd told him she didn't want to see him, and he wasn't going to beg.

So he'd given up on her and finished his degree, then moved to London, trained as a GP, then done a surgical rotation, and now here he was ten years down the line, working for an aid agency in Africa, and still she was following him in his head, in his heart, eating holes in him like some vile flesh-eating bug that wouldn't leave him alone. Asking after him, of all things!

How dare she? How *dare* she ask after him?

And he'd dream about her again tonight, he thought bitterly as he let out the clutch and shot off down the dirt track on the start of his journey. Every time she was mentioned, every time he thought about her, which was pretty much daily, she haunted his sleep, the memory of her laughter, her smile, then those few days and nights they'd had together, so precious, so tender, so absolutely bone-deep *right* that he'd just known she was the only woman he'd ever love—the memories were enough to drive him mad.

As mad as his mother, if she thought he was ever going back to Penhally to expose himself to that again. No way. It would kill him. But just to see her again—to touch her—to hold her in his arms, to bury his nose in her hair and smell the warm summer fragrance that was Gemma…

So he wasn't concentrating when he swerved off the

road to avoid the broken-down car. He wasn't thinking that it was strange for the car to be there, that it was possibly a booby trap. He wasn't looking out for the rebels who'd left it there to trick him into going onto the verge.

He was thinking about his wife, about the soft sighs, the taste of her skin, the sobbing screams as she came apart in his arms.

And then he hit the landmine.

CHAPTER ONE

'HERE'S trouble.'

Gemma looked up from the paperwork she was sorting and saw old Doris Trefusis jerk her head towards the door. And her heart hiccuped against her ribs, because there could be only one person she was talking about, and she wasn't ready!

How silly. She'd thought she was prepared, but apparently not, if the pounding of her heart and the shaking of her legs was anything to go by.

Since his mother's stroke yesterday evening, she'd been psyching herself up for Sam coming down from London, but nothing could have prepared her for the emotional impact of her first sight of him in years. Ten years, nine months, two weeks, three days and four and a half hours, to be exact.

Long, lonely years in which she'd ached for him, hungry for any scrap of news, any snippet that would tell her what he was up to. Then last year his distraught mother had told her he'd been hurt in a stupid bike accident and she'd misunderstood and thought for a fleeting second that he'd died. Not for long, but it had devastated her, the pain of loss slamming through her and bringing home to her just how much she still loved him.

But that was ridiculous, because she didn't know him, not any more—if she ever really had. They'd been little more than kids, but he wasn't a kid now. Lord, no.

Not that he'd really been one then, at nineteen, but he certainly wasn't now, she thought, her heart lurching as he came into view. She was standing in the shadows at the back of Reception and she watched spellbound as he sauntered in, tall and broad, more solid than he had been in his late teens, but every bit as gorgeous. A slight limp was the only sign of his injuries, if anything only adding another layer of attraction, and that cocky smile flickering round his mouth was tearing her composure to shreds. But it wasn't for her. He hadn't seen her yet in her shadowy corner, and his smile was for Mrs Trefusis.

'Morning, Doris!' he said, and his deep, husky voice, so painfully familiar, made her heart turn over. 'How are you? Looking as young and gorgeous as ever, I see!'

Their diminutive and elderly cleaner put the magazines she was tidying back in the rack and looked him up and down, her mouth pursed repressively even though her eyes were twinkling. 'Good morning, Dr Cavendish.'

Gemma saw his mouth twitch and his eyebrows shoot up. '*Dr Cavendish*? Whatever happened to young Samuel? I get the feeling I'm still in trouble with you, Doris—or does it have to be Mrs Trefusis now?'

Doris tutted. 'You can hardly expect a warm welcome, Samuel. You've been gone so long, and your poor mother—'

He snorted. 'My poor mother has had my support

continuously since my father walked out seventeen years ago, as you very well know.'

'From a distance. You should have been here, Sam,' she chided gently.

Did his smile lose its sparkle? Maybe, although it didn't waver as he went on, 'Well, I'm here now, so you can start by offering me a cup of tea. I'm as dry as a desert.'

Doris sniffed. 'I'm not sure you deserve one.'

He grinned and gave her a slow, lazy wink. 'You're just saying that. You love me really,' he said, and Gemma watched old Doris Trefusis melt under the megawatt charm.

'Go away with you,' she said, blushing and flapping her hand at him. 'I'll bring it in—Dr Tremayne's half expecting you. I might even be able to find you one of Hazel's fairings if those doctors have left you any. She made an extra batch specially when she knew you were coming home.'

'What, to help lure me back in?' he said drily, glancing at Hazel Furse, the practice manager, with a wry smile. Then, as if he'd only just become aware of her presence at the back of Reception, he turned and met Gemma's eyes, his face suddenly expressionless.

'Gemma.'

That was all, just the one word, but it stopped her heart in its tracks. *Oh, Sam. Were your eyes always so blue? Like a Mediterranean sky at night, cobalt blue, piercing through me.*

'Hello, Sam.' Her voice sounded forced, and she had to swallow the sudden lump of emotion in her throat. 'Welcome home.'

His jaw tightened, and he nodded. 'Thank you.

Hopefully it won't be for too long. Mrs Furse, would you be kind enough to tell Dr T. I'm here, please.'

'Sam! Good to see you! I saw you drive up. Come on in. Doris, I don't know if you could rustle up some tea…'

'It's all in hand, Dr Tremayne. Kettle's already on.'

Without another word to her, Sam turned his back on Gemma and limped into Nick's surgery, the older man's arm slung round his shoulders, and the door closed behind them.

She let her breath out then, unaware that she'd been holding it ever since he'd come in, holding back a part of herself that was too vulnerable, too tender and delicate and scarred to let him see.

He was back. Sam was back, but not the way she'd always dreamed of, had waited breathlessly for ever since she'd returned to Penhally last year in the hope that he might find out she was here and come back to her. Instead he'd come back for yet another family crisis, another duty visit, another call on his endless good nature and sense of responsibility that nobody else ever seemed to recognise.

But he hadn't come back for her, and she realised now, after seeing him, after the way he'd looked at her, that he never would. And the pain was devastating…

'Are you all right?'

She opened her eyes and saw Kate Althorp, one of their midwives, watching her with concern in her all-too-intelligent eyes.

'I'm fine, Kate.'

'Are you sure? You look a little pale.'

'I'm fine,' she said again, more firmly, because if Kate didn't let her go and get on, she was going to do something stupid like burst into tears in Reception. And there was no way she was letting anyone see her show so much as a flicker of emotion.

Even if her heart was being torn in two…

Sam stood at the window and stared back along Harbour Road at the devastation left behind by the flood last autumn, putting Gemma's face out of his mind. 'What happened to the Anchor Hotel?' he asked, although in truth he didn't care. It and its patrons had never appealed to him, and he was sure it had been mutual.

'It's been demolished—the new additions that were never properly built—and they're rebuilding it. There were a lot of properties damaged around the bottom of Bridge Street and Gull Close. There are lots of people still out of their homes.'

'It must have been quite something.'

'It was. It's a miracle the bridge survived. The noise was tremendous.'

'I'm sure. I missed all the news, I'm afraid—I was in hospital.'

'Yes, I know, your mother said you'd had an accident on your bike. I see you're still limping a bit. How are you?'

'Really?' He shrugged. 'Better. Frustrated by the slow progress, but better. So—I gather your crew are all married now?' he said, changing the subject to one he was more comfortable with, and Nick smiled, his lean face relaxing slightly.

'Yes, they are. And Jack and Lucy have both got families. In fact Lucy's decided she doesn't want to come back, so there's a job here if you're at a loose end…'

Sam snorted softly and shook his head at his old friend and mentor. 'I owe you a great deal, Dr T., but not that much.' Not while his wife was working here. 'Anyway, I'll be busy.'

'Yes, of course. How is your mother? She was pretty bad when I saw her yesterday evening, on her way in, but I phoned this morning and they said she's doing well.'

'Yes, she is, thanks. They've got her in the specialist stroke unit, and they scanned her straight away and put her on mega clot-busters, and she's improving already.'

'That's excellent. We're lucky to have the stroke unit. It's a real asset, but she'll still need some support for a while. Is that going to be a problem for you?'

'Not really.' He'd spent the last few months torn between physio and a desk job he loathed, trying to earn his keep at the charity he'd been working for when he'd been blown up and wondering where the hell to go from here. Next to all of that, this further infringement of his personal choice was small potatoes.

But his mother's life—well, that was certainly going to change, and if she had her way, change his with it. 'She's OK,' he said, trying to sound convincing. 'It's her left side, mostly her hand and her face, but that's just the visible stuff. I have no idea what else might have been affected or what she'll get back with this intensive treatment. Hopefully she'll make a full recovery, but I expect the full extent will reveal itself in time. I would have thought there are bound to be some after-effects.'

'Any idea of the cause?'

He shook his head. 'Not as yet. They're looking into it—she's having an echocardiogram and a carotid scan, and she's on a monitor, but so far they've drawn a blank. Her blood pressure's dreadful, too, and she's put on weight. Her diet's always been atrocious—she's addicted to chocolate, always has been, and the only reason she isn't enormous is that she hardly eats anything else. God alone knows what Jamie's been surviving on, there's no food in the house to speak of, and she's obviously depressed.'

'We'll sort her out, Sam, once she's home. Don't worry. And how's your brother coping?'

Sam turned away from the window and eased into a chair with a sigh, toying with one of Hazel's biscuits. 'By running away from it, I think, but he's been worrying her for a while. He's a nightmare. It's all too familiar, I'm afraid. Been there, done that, as the saying goes. I gather he's in trouble with the police as well, just to add insult to injury.'

'He is. He's got in with a bad crowd—Gary Lovelace amongst others.'

Sam frowned. 'Lovelace?'

'Yes—do you remember him? Proper little tearaway as a child, and he's no better now. He's a year older than Jamie, I think.'

He trawled his brains. 'I remember the name—probably the father's. Always in and out of the slammer for one thing or another. Petty stuff mostly, if I remember. So Gary's leading my little brother astray, is he? Damn.'

'I think he's willing to be led,' Nick said wryly. 'I've tried, Sam. I can't get through to him. I don't know him like I knew you—because my children have all grown up now, I hardly see his generation, whereas you were always in the house—usually in the kitchen eating us out of house and home or getting up to mischief in the garden. I can remember a few spontaneous bonfires…'

He gave Nick a crooked grin over the rim of his mug. 'Hmm. My "SAS" phase. Sorry about that.'

'Don't be sorry. You never really did any harm, and you were always welcome. Annabel had a really soft spot for you, you know.'

He met Nick's eyes with a pensive smile. 'I was very fond of her. You must miss her.'

'I do. She was a good woman. She used to worry about you, you know, and how your mother relied on you so heavily. It was no wonder you went off the rails. You had more than enough on your plate.'

'Yeah, well, that doesn't change, does it? I can't believe I'm back picking up the pieces all over again.'

'I can. You were a good boy, and you've turned into a good man, just as I knew you would.'

'Oh, that's just so much bull, Nick, and you know it. I wouldn't be here at all if I had the slightest damned excuse to get away.'

'Yes, you would—and your mother needs you. She misses you. Lots of people do.'

He gave a wry snort. 'Hardly. They all remember me as a hell-raiser. Even Doris Trefusis tore me off a strip on the way in, and I have no doubt Audrey Baxter won't waste a moment telling me I'm not welcome home.'

'Ah, no—you'll be spared that one. Mrs Baxter died in the flood.'

'Really? Poor woman.' He gave a wry smile. 'Not that she'd say that about me. She was always horrible to me—she made damn sure everyone knew everything I ever did, to the point that I used to do things in front of her and place bets with myself that my mother would know before I got home.'

'You were just misunderstood.'

He wasn't so sure about that. He grunted and looked around, not wanting to get into the past he was so keen to avoid. 'So—what's going on here? It looks a bit different to the last time I saw it. I haven't been in here since I did work experience when your brother was the GP.'

'Well, it's certainly changed since then. We reopened it five years ago.' He paused, his face troubled, and Sam realised he looked suddenly a great deal older. As well he might. Then he seemed to pull himself together and stood up. 'Come and have a look round. I doubt if you'll recognise it now. We've extended out the back, built a new minor injuries unit and X-ray and plaster rooms, but we're also planning to build another extension on the side into what used to be Althorps'. The boatyard burned down in September, and it worked in our favour because we were able to buy part of the site—do you remember Kate Althorp? James's widow?'

'Vaguely. I know the name and I remember James dying in the storm.'

A quick frown flitted across Nick's brow. 'Yes. Well, her brother-in-law wanted to sell up, and without the income Kate's half was redundant, so they cashed in on the insurance and sold the site. We bought enough land at the side of the surgery to extend it further, and to provide some more consulting rooms so we can extend the facilities offered by the MIU, which will give us a much better use of our space here. Come and see. You'll be impressed, I hope.'

He was—but he wasn't fooled. Nick was angling, but Sam wasn't biting. Under any other circumstances—but they weren't. They were what they were, and what they were was too damned hard to contemplate. They were standing at the top of the stairs discussing Nick's vision for the future of the surgery as a multi-disciplinary health centre with dental and osteopathy services when Nick was called to the phone, and he left Sam there and went into a consulting room to take the call.

And Gemma, who'd been the one to find Nick and tell him he was wanted on the phone, was left standing there with Sam, her soft grey-blue eyes wary, her body language defensive. As if he was in some way a threat.

That was a laugh. She was far more of a threat to him than he would ever be to her. She was the one who'd walked away.

He held her eyes, hardening himself to the expression in them, refusing to be drawn in. 'My mother said you were back.'

'Yes, I've been working here for a year now. How is she, Sam? Nick said she was improving.'

'Doing really well. Rather shocked, I think. We all are. She's only fifty-seven.'

'I know, but she's had high blood pressure for years, and her diet's a bit lacking.'

'What, in anything other than chocolate?' he said with a wry grin, and then felt his heart turn over when she smiled back. Oh, God, he wanted her—wanted to haul her into his arms, up against his chest and bury his nose in that thick, soft waterfall of hair, to breathe her in and see if she still smelled the same.

'She said you're still single,' he told her with an edge to his voice, and the smile faded instantly as she looked away.

'Well, we both know that's not true,' she said under her breath.

'I never could work it out. All this time, and you haven't asked for a divorce. And I wonder why not.'

'Well, you haven't, either.'

'No. It's not really been an issue. I've been busy.' Busy trying to forget her, busy pretending to himself that he didn't need a social life, that his marriage was just on hold and one day…

'I gathered. In Africa, saving the world. So how did you fall off this bike?'

'Oh, you know me—always taking risks, pushing my luck, playing the fool.'

'You're thirty, Sam. Isn't it time you grew up and stopped worrying your mother sick?'

He swallowed. Oh, he was grown up. He'd grown up the day he'd come home late from work with a bunch of flowers for her and found her letter.

Nick returned from taking his call. 'Sorry about that. Right, where were we?'

'I'll leave you to it. Send Linda my love,' Gemma said, and fled back into her room, her heart pounding, her legs like jelly and her stupid, stupid hormones racing through her body and dragging it from an eleven-year slumber into vibrant, screaming wakefulness…

'So—what do you think of the set-up?'

Nick had concluded his guided tour after a walk through the minor injuries suite downstairs and a quick chat with Lauren, the physio, a local girl whom Sam vaguely remembered, and they were back in Reception when Nick asked the question, his expression hopeful despite the simple words.

Except of course there was nothing simple about them, and it didn't take a genius to read the sub-text.

'Excellent—but I'm not falling for it, Nick,' Sam said softly. 'I don't want to work here.' Not with Gemma.

'Why? You need a job, we need a doctor. Your mother and brother need you and, frankly, looking at you, I reckon you need us. Can't I talk you into it—at least for a few weeks until we can get someone to take over? We'd be hugely grateful, and it would give you something productive to do while your mother recovers.'

'I've got plenty to do. The garden can't have been touched for years—'

'Gardening leave?' Nick said softly, his eyes mocking. 'At least think about it. Maybe it's time to come home, Sam.'

But then Gemma came downstairs again, and their eyes locked and pain lanced through him.

'I don't think so,' he muttered, and, turning on his heel, he crossed the reception area in two strides and slapped the swing door out of his way.

Then and only then did he breathe again...

She didn't know how she got through the rest of the day.

Sam had left the building, but his aura hung in the air, his presence filling every corner and bringing a huge lump to her throat every time she allowed herself the luxury of thinking of him.

Not that she had much time, because she had a busy afternoon surgery and afterwards she was due to go up to the high school for a careers evening. And on her way home to change, of course, she had to drive past his mother's house, and his car was on the drive. At least she assumed it was his car, because it had a hire-car logo in the window.

Oh, why was she so fixated on him? She couldn't afford to let herself do this. He was passing through, doing what he'd done over and over again, coming back only for long enough to do what was necessary and this time, just for good measure, tearing the scab off her wounded heart.

If she let him. She didn't have to, of course. She could keep him firmly at a distance. She'd heard Nick ask him to stay, seen him leave the building as if it were on fire.

Sam wouldn't be staying.

And she wouldn't be letting him into her heart.

'Sam! Hello, darling, I hoped you'd come.'

'Hiya. How are you? You sound better—your speech is much clearer. That's fantastic.' He brushed a kiss over his mother's drooping cheek—was it less noticeable?—and eased himself down into the chair beside her bed. 'I've brought you some grapes.'

'Not chocolate?'

He gave a short laugh. 'No, Mum, not chocolate. Grapes are good for you and, besides, I like them.' He helped himself to a handful and settled back in the chair, one foot crossed over the other knee. 'Anyway, I want to talk to you. About Jamie.'

'Oh, Sam, where is he?' she slurred, her eyes welling. 'I thought you'd bring him.'

'No, sorry, I had to walk the dog, and when I got back he'd gone out—he sent me a text, though. He had to be at school, he said.'

'He doesn't want to see me.'

He didn't tell her that the thought had occurred to him, too. 'No, it's legit. I rang the school—it's a careers evening and he's apparently volunteered to help out. I'm going over there as soon as I leave you to make sure he's there and talk to the staff.'

'Oh, dear,' she said ruefully.

'Mmm. I'm sure they'll have lots to say, but so have I. Don't worry, I'll sort Jamie out. You just concentrate on getting better.'

She gave a funny little laugh, then her face creased. 'How's Digger? Does he miss me?'

Sam smiled. 'I think he does, but he's enjoying his walks. We had a lovely run on the beach this morning at dawn.' Down to the other beach, to sit on the stumps of the old cabin and torture himself with the memories…

'Don't let him off the lead. He'll go down a hole.'

Sam laughed softly. 'I do remember you telling me how he got his name. I'll keep him on the lead, don't worry.'

'So—did you go to the surgery?' she asked after the slightest pause, and he braced himself for the inevitable questions.

'Yes, I saw Nick.'

'And Gemma?'

He felt his mouth tighten and consciously relaxed it. 'Yes, I saw Gemma. She sends her love. She seems to know you quite well.'

'Oh, she does. She runs the cont…'

She trailed off, exasperated by her uncooperative tongue, and Sam put in, 'The continuing care clinic?'

'Mmm. She does my blood pressure. She's beautiful, isn't she? Pretty girl.'

'I didn't notice,' he lied. 'I was a bit busy.'

God, it was a wonder his nose wasn't longer than Pinocchio's! He put the grapes back on his mother's bed table before he crushed them all inadvertently, moved her newspaper and picked up her weakened left hand.

'Come on, let's do some physio. We need to keep these fingers moving.'

She shook her head. 'They just won't.'

'They will. Keep trying. Here, come on, I'll help you,' he said, and, taking her fingers in his, he started working on them, giving himself something to do apart from conjuring Gemma's image into his crazed mind.

But it didn't work, her image was still there larger than life, her soft, wounded, wary eyes torturing him, so after a few minutes he put his mother's hand down and stood up. 'Right, I'm off to the school to sort out young Jamie. I'll see you tomorrow. Be good.'

'What else?' she said sadly, and her eyes filled again, ripping at his conscience. 'Bring him—come for longer. I miss you, Sam. You don't know…'

His conscience stabbed him again, and he sighed softly. 'I do. You tell me often enough. But my life's not here, Mum.'

'Could be.'

'No. No, it couldn't. Just the moment you're better and I'm given the all-clear by the physios, I'm going back to Africa.'

Her fingers tightened on his, her right hand clutching at him in desperation. 'No, Sam! Don't! You can't go back!'

That was probably true, although not the way she meant it, but he wasn't giving in. Not yet. 'Mum, I have to go,' he repeated, and, freeing his hand, he dropped a swift kiss on her cheek and walked out.

'Sam! I didn't expect to see you here. It's ne last place!'

'Well, ditto,' he said, and his smile looked strained. 'Have you seen Jamie?'

'He's here somewhere,' Gemma said, trying to control her see-sawing emotions. 'Doing the name badges and the drinks for the parents? He will have done the careers thing last year, so he's only helping. I don't like to be unkind, but it doesn't sound like him.'

'Maybe it was just a reason not to go and see Mum. He hasn't been in yet. I think he's scared, but while I'm here I need to speak to his teachers and find out what I can about him hanging around with Gary Lovelace.'

'Well, Lachlan D'Ancey's here, he'll fill you in. He's Chief Constable now, but he just comes to support the school and sell the police force. Nick Tremayne's here, too. If Lachlan's busy I expect Nick could use some help, there are always lots of people thinking of studying medicine.'

He shook his head. 'I don't think the school would be interested in my support. I wasn't exactly their star pupil.'

'That's rubbish, Sam, you got four As at A level!'

'Only because I was constantly being grounded.'

She smiled slightly, remembering the tales of how rebellious he'd been, how he'd pushed everyone to the limit of their patience, worried his mother senseless and alienated half of the town.

Which, of course, had only made him even more attractive.

She dragged her eyes from Sam and looked at the girl who was hovering behind him. 'Hi. Did you want to see me?'

'Um—yes, please. I'm thinking of going into nursing, and I wondered if you could tell me about it.'

Out of the corner of her eye she saw Sam lift his hand in farewell as he walked away, and she stifled a sigh of regret.

Foolish, foolish woman. It's over. Forget it.

But she couldn't, and for the rest of the evening her eyes were constantly searching for him, and every time they found him, her silly, stupid heart would lurch against her ribs.

It might be over, but apparently she couldn't forget it. Not for the last nearly eleven years, and certainly not now, with Sam right here under her nose, his presence reminding her of everything she'd lost…

CHAPTER TWO

'SAM—good to see you.'

He stifled a wry grin at the blatant lie from the man who'd had altogether too much to do with him in his youth. 'Hello, Lachlan. How are you?'

'Very well. Great, actually. Married again.'

Sam hadn't known he'd got unmarried, but he wasn't surprised that yet another thing had happened in Penhally without him knowing. He'd done his best to distance himself, so it was hardly rocket science, and he made some trite and socially acceptable remark and then Lachlan brought the conversation, not unexpectedly, around to Jamie.

'Your brother's getting himself in a bit of bother these days,' he murmured. 'You want to have a word with him. He's going to end up with a criminal record if he goes on like this, and it's a crying shame because he's a good lad really. Sharp as a tack, which is half his trouble, of course, like it was yours. What he needs is a good role model.'

'Well, don't look at me,' Sam said with a low laugh. 'I'm the last person to give him advice.'

'I disagree. You're just the person—he reminds me a lot of you.'

'What—loud and unruly?'

'No—lost,' he said, and Sam looked away, uncomfortable with Lachlan's all too accurate interpretation of his youthful emotions. 'You need to get him out of the influence of that young Gary Lovelace. He's a nasty piece of work—God alone knows what Jamie sees in him, but he's leading your little brother into all sorts of mischief.'

Sam straightened. 'Not drugs?'

'Not that we know of, but I shouldn't be surprised. But Gary's a thief, and a bully, like his father and his little brother, and you need to get Jamie away from him before something bad happens.'

Sam sighed inwardly. This was the last thing he needed.

'So how's your mother? I was sorry to hear about her stroke—she seems far too young.'

'Yes. But strokes can happen to anyone, from tiny babies upwards. She's making great progress, but we just need to know why it happened to stop it happening again.'

'You ought to speak to Gemma. It was Gemma who found her. She went round after work and checked up on her because she was worried.'

'Did she?' he said softly, wondering why Gemma hadn't mentioned it. Because she didn't want to talk to him any more than she had to? Very likely. He didn't really want to talk to her, either, and so far all their exchanges had been carefully contained, with all hell breaking loose just under the surface—at least, on his side. But if Gemma had found his mother, she could easily have been responsible for saving her life, and at the very least he ought to thank her. Not even he was that churlish.

'I'll go and have a word. Thanks, Lachlan—and if you hear anything I need to know about Jamie, let me know.'

'Will do. And you do the same.'

'Sure.'

He went back towards Gemma, but there was a crowd of young girls around her, so he wandered over to the desk where Jamie was handing out name tags and soft drinks to parents.

'Checking up on me?' Jamie said, his mouth set in a defiant line, and Sam just smiled.

'No. I don't need to, I've got the rest of Penhally doing that, by all accounts. How long are you going to be here?'

'Another few minutes, then I'm going out with my friends.'

Sam frowned. 'Why? It's a school night. You've got your exams in a few weeks, you should be working.'

'Nah. I've got it all under control, Sam. You don't have to come home and play the heavy brother with me.'

'That's not what I'm hearing.'

'Well, tough. What do they know?'

'Well, I gather Mr D'Ancey knows quite a lot about you—probably rather more than is healthy.'

Jamie's eyes slid away and his face took on a defensive cast. 'Whatever. I'm out tonight. My work's up to date, I've got nothing outstanding—and don't even think about suggesting I tidy my bedroom. All I hear from Mum is that I'm just like you.'

Sam stifled a smile and gave up—for now. 'OK. But not late. Ten.'

'Ten-thirty.'

'Ten-fifteen—and if you're so much as thirty seconds late, you're grounded for a week.'

'What? Where do you get off—?'

'Suit yourself. Ten-fifteen or you're grounded. I'll see you later.'

And without giving his brother a chance to argue any further, he walked away. Gemma was free now, and he crossed to her quickly before another wannabe nurse appeared. 'Can we talk?'

Her eyes widened with alarm, and he realised she'd misunderstood. Or maybe she hadn't, not really, but he wasn't getting into all that now. He could barely keep a lid on his emotions as it was. The last thing he needed was to have a deeply personal conversation in public with the woman who'd shredded his heart. 'About my mother,' he added, and saw the alarm recede.

'Sure. When are you thinking of?'

'After you finish? I haven't eaten yet, I don't know if you have, but I thought we could go up to the Smugglers' and have something there while we talk.'

She nodded slowly. 'That would be fine. Give me another few minutes, and if nobody else comes, we can go.'

'Fine.' He gave her a brisk nod, and walked off to find Nick.

'Ah, Sam, just the man. This is Dr Cavendish—he's been working in Africa with an aid agency—was it Doctors Without Borders?'

'No, but it's similar,' he said. 'Why?'

'Young David here is considering medicine and wants to work in that field. Can you give him some advice?'

He dredged up a smile for the youngster. 'Sure. What do you want to know?'

'Sorry about that, I got caught up.'

'So did I. Nick found me a young lad with a death

wish. He wants to work in Africa—he's talking about doing a gap year with an aid agency before he goes to med school.'

'So what did you say?'

'Don't do it. Are you all done now?'

'Yes.'

'Then let's get out of here—have you got your car?'

'Yes. Shall I meet you up at the pub?'

'Good idea.'

He followed her down past the surgery to the harbour and turned right along Harbour Road past the shrouded site of the Anchor Hotel, over the River Lanson at the bottom of Bridge Street and along to the end, past Nick Tremayne's house and his mother's house next door, then up the hill, past the little church on the left with the lighthouse beyond it on the headland, and then over the rise to the Smugglers' Inn.

The place was doing well, if the number of cars outside on a week night was anything to go by, and he parked in the last space and got out, breathing deeply and drawing the fresh sea air into his lungs.

God, that smelt good. It was one of the few things about Penhally that he missed—apart from Gemma, who was walking towards him now, her eyes unreadable in the dimly lit car park. Her hands were stuffed into the pockets of her coat, and she looked wary and uncertain, as if she was regretting saying yes.

She didn't need to. He wasn't a threat to her. He had no intention of getting into any personal territory at all. Not even slightly.

'Lots of cars,' he said, aiming for something neutral. 'Do you think we'll get a seat?'

She looked round and shrugged. 'I don't know. We

could always sit outside on the terrace,' she said doubtfully.

Hell, no. They'd spent whole evenings on that terrace, and it was the last place he wanted to go. 'It's not warm enough, the food might get cold.'

'There might be room inside.'

'We'll see.' Oh, God, endless pleasantries, and all he really wanted to do was touch her, thread her hair through his fingers, feel her body soft against his...

He yanked open the door of the pub and ushered her in, and as they walked into the bar, a hush fell.

'Well, by all the saints, young Samuel. Come home to cause havoc, have 'e, lad?'

'Ignore him,' Gemma muttered, but he went over to old Fred Spencer and shook his hand.

'How are you, Mr Spencer?'

'Better'n you, by all accounts. Why you limpin'?'

'Fell off my bike,' he said economically. 'And don't say it.'

'Well, I 'spect it *was* your fault.'

'Why not? It always was, wasn't it?'

The old man cracked a laugh and turned back to his companions. 'Always had to have the last word, young Sam.'

Only not always. Not with Gemma. There'd been no chance to have the last word, to talk things through, to get to the bottom of it—and he wasn't starting now.

Leaving Fred with his mates, they went over to the bar and ordered drinks and scanned the specials board.

'The steak's still good,' Gemma said. 'I think I'll have that—just the small one.'

'Rare?'

She nodded, surprised and yet not that he would have

remembered. They'd always had the steak frites in here, and it had always been good, and she'd always had it rare.

Listen to her! Always, indeed. What was she thinking? It had only been—what? Ten, maybe twelve times in all, over more than a year? But it was all the time they'd had together, and it had been precious, every last second of it.

He ordered the steak for her, but to her surprise he ordered beef Stroganoff for himself—just in case she thought it was all too cosy down Memory Lane? She wasn't sure, not sure at all, about any of it, and she didn't really have any idea what she was doing here with him, tearing herself apart, when she could have been safely tucked up at home.

'Ah, there's a table here,' he said, and led her across the room to where a couple were just leaving. He held the chair for her to sit down, and as he did so, his hand brushed her arm.

Dear God, he thought, desperately resisting the need to touch her again, to reach out and let his fingers linger over that soft, slender arm, to run them over her shoulder, to slide the lightweight jersey top aside and press his lips to her skin…

He retreated to the safety of the other side of the table and sat down opposite her, flicking his eyes over the menu even though he'd already ordered, staring out of the window as she shuffled in her seat, organising her bag, placing her drink carefully in the centre of the beer mat with great precision.

And then, once they were settled and there was nothing left to fidget with, there was a silence that was so full of unspoken words it was like a roar in his head. And he had to break it or go mad.

'So—you came back to Penhally,' he said, trying to find something neutral to talk about and failing dismally at the first hurdle.

She glanced away, but not before he'd seen a shadow in her eyes. 'Yes. I love it here.'

Especially when he wasn't there. His mouth tipped in a mocking smile. 'I thought it was too small for you? Too pedestrian. Too provincial. Wasn't that why you left to see the world and didn't come back?'

Hardly. It was the place where her heart was, where she'd found a love she'd thought would last forever, but she couldn't tell him that or she'd have to tell him why she'd gone, so she just gave him a level look and lied in her teeth.

'You know why I left—to go travelling while I considered my career options. And you can talk about leaving to see the world, Sam. It's me who's living here now. You've hardly been home.'

'*Et tu, Brute*? Isn't this where you tell me that I've failed my mother and failed my brother and ought to move home like a good little boy? Well, news flash, Gemma. I've got a life now, and it's not here. And it never will be.' Thanks to her. His jaw tightened, and she felt a stab of pain for him, and for herself.

'I'm sorry,' she said softly. 'It's none of my business. But for what it's worth, I don't think you should come home for your mother or your brother. You did more than enough for them, Sam, and you've got two sisters who don't live a million miles away who could be putting more into this than they are. But maybe you should think about coming home for you.'

'Oh, for God's sake, what *is* it about Penhally and everyone telling me what to do?'

'I wasn't telling you—'

'Weren't you? Well, it sounded like it from where I'm sitting.'

Or maybe that was his conscience, he thought, guilt racking him yet again for the hurt look he'd put in her eyes.

'I don't want to go into this. I brought you here to talk about my mother's stroke, not me,' he said after a moment in which they'd both taken a deep breath and regrouped. 'I gather you found her last night?'

She met his eyes squarely, her own still reproachful. 'Yes—she came in the day before yesterday to see me for a routine blood-pressure check, and she mentioned that she'd noticed her heart doing something funny in the evening a couple of times. I had a word with Adam—Adam Donnelly, one of our doctors—and he suggested we should do an ECG and then refer her to St Piran for some tests.'

'And?'

'I did the ECG yesterday, and there was nothing out of the ordinary at all, but I was just a bit worried about her. Her blood pressure was up again, and—I don't know, she just didn't seem right. And she looked a bit strained around the eyes. So after work I popped in. There was no reply to the doorbell, so I went round the back and opened the door because I could hear Digger whining, and I found her at the kitchen table, looking chalky grey and sweaty and feeling terrible. And she had a killer headache, apparently, and she said she'd had some kind of convulsion, but I noticed her mouth was drooping a bit and then she just lost her speech. It was a classic stroke, so I called Nick and got the ambulance on its way, and alerted the specialist unit, and—well, I

don't know how she is now. I went in with her last night
because Jamie wasn't around and I didn't want her to
be alone, but I haven't had time to get up there again. I
was going to go and see her in my lunch break but I
thought you might be there, and then there was the
careers evening so I just haven't had a chance. So how
is she? Really? She must have been so frightened.'

He nodded slowly. 'I think so. But who wouldn't be?
It's a really big thing, isn't it, and it could have been so
much worse if you hadn't checked on her. I hate to
think what would have happened if you hadn't. It
sounds as if your prompt action's made a huge difference to the impact of her stroke, and if you hadn't gone
in—well, talking to the staff it's clear that without im-
mediate help she could easily have died, so thank you.
She sends you her love, by the way. She seems very
fond of you.'

Gemma gave a soft, wry little laugh. 'I can't imagine
why. I bully her dreadfully.'

'She needs it. So—about this heart thing…'

'Mmm. I mean, obviously it hasn't been investigated
properly yet, but I was wondering—do you think she
could have some kind of AF?'

'Atrial fibrillation? Could well be. It would fit. I just
can't understand how she hasn't felt it in her chest
before, if she's got AF and it's sustained enough that
she's forming clots. You'd think you'd feel it if your
heart's not beating right.'

'Not everyone does feel it, though, and atrial fibrillation is notoriously tricky to control.'

'Especially if you OD on stimulants like tea and
coffee and very dark chocolate. It's always given her the
odd palpitation, and maybe it's just accustomed her to

a funny heartbeat from time to time, and then the AF doesn't feel so very different—'

'Steak frites and beef Stroganoff?'

'Thanks, Tony,' Sam said, leaning back so the landlord could put their plates down. He paused to welcome Sam back.

'Good to see you again. How are things? Sorry about your mother.'

'Thanks,' he said, feeling a little awkward because clearly everyone knew about her, recognised him and also recognised the fact that he'd been notable by his absence. Then he chatted to Gemma for a few moments, and while he listened to them, Sam watched her, her face attentive, her eyes crinkling with humour when Tony made a joke, and all the time her lips were moving, soft and warm, bare of lipstick but moist from the occasional flick of her tongue, and it was getting increasingly difficult to sit there and pretend that he felt nothing for her, this woman who'd torn his heart apart.

His wife, for heaven's sake.

Then Tony moved away, and he turned his attention to his food, and for a while they were both silent. Then she lifted her head and said, 'You know you made that remark about David having a death wish because he wanted to go to Africa? What did you mean?'

He shrugged. 'It was just a joke.'

'No. You meant something, and you said you'd told him not to go, and when you were talking to Fred just now about the accident—what happened, Sam?' she asked softly. 'Did you really just fall off your bike?'

He sighed and set down his fork. 'Really? In a manner of speaking,' he said, and then bluntly, because he still wanted to lash out, he went on, 'I hit a landmine.'

Her face bleached of colour, and he caught her glass just as it slipped through her fingers. 'Careful, anybody would think you still cared, and we all know that's not true,' he said with bitter irony.

She sat back, her eyes filling, and closed them quickly, but not quickly enough because a single tear slipped down her cheek and that old guilt thing kicked in again. 'Actually I was thinking of your mother—how she would have coped if…'

'If I'd died?' he prompted, trying not to look at the tear, and she sucked in a tiny breath.

'Don't.' She swallowed and opened her eyes, reaching for her glass. He still had it in his hand, and as he passed it to her, their fingers met and he felt the shock race through him again.

Damn. Still, after all these years…

She took a sip and put it down, then met his eyes again. 'So what really happened, Sam? With the landmine?'

He made himself concentrate on something other than the little trail the tear had made on her cheek. 'There was a booby trap—a car in the road. I swerved round it, not paying attention, and the back wheel caught the anti-personnel mine and it hurled the back of the bike up into the air. Luckily the panniers were rammed with equipment, which protected me from the blast, but the force of the explosion threw me forwards onto the ground.'

'And?'

'And I broke my collar bone and my ankle,' he told her, grossly oversimplifying it. 'Oh, and tore the rotator cuff in my left shoulder.'

She nodded slowly. 'I've noticed you don't use your left hand very much.'

'Got out of the habit,' he lied, and turned his attention back to his food, leaving her sitting there in silence, struggling with the image of him being hurled through the air and smashed into the ground.

She felt sick. It could have been so much worse, she thought, and set down her knife and fork, unable to eat while her emotions churned round inside her and the man she loved was just a foot away, his eyes fixed on his plate, obviously in a hurry now to finish his meal and leave. He'd only wanted to thank her for finding his mother, and he'd done that, and now he just wanted to go.

Fair enough. So did she, and she was about to get up and leave when Tony stopped by their table.

'Everything all right?' he asked, and she nodded and smiled at him and picked up her knife and fork again, forcing herself to finish her food before it was not only the flavour of sawdust, but stone cold with it.

'So how long will she be in?' he asked the registrar the next day.

'Just a few days. We want to get her anticoagulation sorted and then she can be discharged.'

He felt a flicker of fear, the tightening of the noose of responsibility, and consciously slowed his breathing down.

'Surely she can't come home until she's able to look after herself?'

'But I gather you're at home now, so that's not a problem, is it?'

He arched a brow. 'You want me to look after my mother? Attend to her personal care?'

'Why not? You're a doctor.'

But she's my *mother*! he wanted to scream, but it was

pointless. She would have done the same for him, and it was only because it made him feel trapped that he was so desperate to get away. And last night, with Gemma— well, it had been an emotional minefield every bit as dangerous to his health as the one he'd encountered on the bike, and he hadn't been able to get away from the pub quick enough.

He'd used Digger as an excuse, and he'd gone back to the house, collected the dog and taken him for a long walk along the beach in the moonlight, right down to the far end and back while he thought about Gemma and how he still wanted her so badly it was tearing holes in him.

He couldn't do it—couldn't stay here. He just wanted to get away, to go back to Africa and lick his wounds in peace. Well, not peace, exactly, but anonymity, at least, without the benefit of the residents of Penhally telling him he'd deserted his mother and let his brother run wild and failed them both, with Gemma in the background reminding him that he'd failed her, too, or why the hell else would she have left him when everything between them had seemed so incredibly perfect?

But he couldn't go back to Africa, because he couldn't operate, because his collar bone hadn't just broken, it had shredded his left brachial plexus and damaged the sensory nerves to his left hand, and his shoulder was still weak from the tear to his rotator cuff when he'd landed on it, and his leg—well, his ankle would heal slowly and improve with time, unlike his hand, but in the meantime he'd struggle to stand for hours operating, even if he could feel what he was doing with his hand, which he couldn't, and he couldn't ride a bike, not with his left arm so compromised and his ankle inflexible, so it was pointless thinking about it and tormenting himself.

And his mother aside, there was the problem of Jamie, who had come in last night at seventeen minutes past ten. Late, but not so late that he was going to say anything, and so they'd established an uneasy truce.

But the need to get away was overwhelming, and after he left the hospital he drove up onto Bodmin Moor and walked for hours with Digger over the rough grass and heather until his ankle was screaming and he wasn't sure how he'd get back, his mind tortured with memories of Gemma, lying there with him in the heather and kissing him back for hour after hour until he thought he'd die of frustration.

Huh. No way. He'd discovered through painful and bitter experience that you didn't die of frustration, you just wished you could, because that would bring an end to it at last.

He sat down on a granite outcrop with the panting Jack Russell at his feet and stared out over the barren, wild landscape while he waited for the pain in his ankle to subside. He could see a few sturdy little ponies grazing and, in the distance, a small herd of Devon Red bullocks turned out for fattening on the spring grass. But apart from that and the inevitable sheep dotted about like cotton-wool balls in the heather, there was nothing there but the wide-open skies and the magical, liquid sound of the curlews.

And gradually, as the warmth of the spring sun seeped into his bones and the bleak, familiar landscape welcomed him home, he accepted what he had to do—what he'd known, ever since he'd had the phone call about her stroke, that he would have to do.

He didn't like it—he didn't like it one bit—but he had no choice, and he would do it, because that was who he was. He would stay at home and look after his mother until she was better, he'd get his brother back on the rails, and then he'd look at his future.

Always assuming he could get off this damned moorland without calling out the Air Ambulance!

'Lauren?'

The physiotherapist looked up and smiled at him a little warily. 'Oh, hi, Sam. How are you?'

He pulled a wry face. 'Sore—that was what I wanted to see you about. I don't suppose I can book myself in for some physio with you, can I? I overdid it up on Bodmin this afternoon and I could do with a good workout. Maybe after you finish one evening?'

Her face clouded. 'Oh. Um—evenings aren't good for me. I've got RP—retinitis pigmentosa…'

She was going blind? 'Hell, I'm sorry, I had no idea.'

She shrugged. 'It's fine, Sam. It's progressing slowly, but I'll take it as it comes and in the meantime—well, I can still do practically everything I did before, but I only work daylight hours now. I can't see very well when the light fades, but I'm more than happy to fit you in at lunchtime—or if Gabriel's not working late so he can get home for the dog, I can do it then if you don't mind giving me a lift home?'

'Of course not—but lunchtime's fine if it suits you best. It's just my ankle.'

'Not your hand and arm?'

He hesitated, glancing down at it and wondering if it was so damned obvious to everyone.

'I noticed you don't use it,' she said gently, 'and you

don't use your shoulder much, either, but it's not obvious, Sam. It's my job—I ought to be able to tell. But it doesn't matter now. Just come and we'll go through it all then, see what I need to do for you. Say—one tomorrow?'

He gave her a fleeting smile. 'That would be great.'

'Can't you keep away, Sam?'

He straightened up and stepped back out of Lauren's doorway, and met the older man's eyes. 'Hi, Nick.'

'So, have you changed your mind? I sincerely hope so. We're so damned busy it's ridiculous. Dragan's out today because the baby was ill and Melinda's had a foul cold and he thinks he's going down with it, too, just to add insult to injury, and everyone in Penhally seems to have realised it's coming up to the spring bank holiday weekend so they're trying to get in quick, and I'm desperately trying to find time to organise the lifeboat barbeque for Saturday. So if you want a job…?'

'Organising the barbeque?' he asked, surprised, but Nick gave a short laugh.

'No, you don't get off that lightly—the locum job.'

He sighed and rammed a hand through his hair. 'Nick, I—'

'Please?'

'I'm out of touch.'

'Rubbish. What the hell do you think you've been doing in Africa?'

He laughed. 'Taking out an appendix under local? Trying to rehydrate a tiny child with boiled river water with some salt flung in it? Lancing an abscess the size of a football? Not juggling someone's drugs to get the best result from their blood-pressure medication, or advising some spoilt middle-aged woman to drink more water, get off her backside and take some exercise if she wants to get rid of her constipation, that's for sure! Hell, Nick, I can't do this any more.'

'Of course you can. Compared to Africa it'll be a walk in the park.'

He shook his head. 'I don't want this, Nick. Don't ask me, please.'

'Why not? It's a great practice, and if you wanted to come back permanently, with Lucy gone I'm sure we can find a slot for you here.' His voice changed, becoming deeper, huskier, and he looked exhausted. 'We're desperate, Sam. We've been struggling without Lucy for weeks, keeping the job open for her because we couldn't get a locum, but now—well, we need to advertise the post and that takes time, and frankly we're all at the end of our rope. We need you.'

Them and everyone else, it seemed. He sighed again and turned away, but there was nowhere to go, because Jamie was running wild and his mother was in hospital and needed him for weeks, if not months, and he couldn't just sit on his backside and watch the world go to hell while he twiddled his thumbs, it just wasn't in his nature. But…

'The people here don't want me, Nick. I was a nightmare.'

'You were a boy. You're a man now. And people forget.'

'Not in Penhally, they don't. They're all bloody elephants.'

Nick chuckled, but his face was still hopeful and he could feel the staff behind the reception desk all holding their breath for his reply.

He shook his head slowly, feeling the ground crumbling beneath his feet. 'OK. I'll help you out—but just the odd day here and there. Nothing drastic. And don't go getting ideas about me coming back in a full-time, permanent post or anything like that, because it just won't happen.'

Nick smiled, slapped him on the shoulder and led him over to Reception. 'Of course not. Hazel, sign him up for locum duty, please. And start booking him in for as much as you can talk him into. I haven't had a day off in four weeks and I'm tired. He can cover Dragan's surgeries tomorrow. Oh, and schedule a practice meeting for the morning—I'll introduce you to everyone, Sam. I'm sure they'll all be delighted you've agreed to join us.'

'Temporarily.'

'Of course, of course,' Nick agreed, but there was something in his voice that wasn't in the least reassuring.

Sam shut his eyes and sighed. Damn.

Damn, damn and double damn.

Why the hell had he said yes?

And then he opened his eyes and saw Gemma staring at him with a stricken look, and if there'd been any way out, he would have taken it.

But there wasn't, and he wasn't any more delighted than she was.

CHAPTER THREE

How on earth was she going to work with him?

She hadn't spoken to him since she'd left the Smugglers' on Wednesday night, and her heart hadn't settled back into a normal rhythm since he'd been back in Penhally. But work with him, having to talk to him about patients, going into the staffroom and finding him sitting there and having to exchange polite conversation when all she wanted to do was turn back the clock and—

What? Not have married him? Not have spent that wonderful, idyllic time with him that fate had so savagely cut short? It would have been kinder, but not to have had that time—even the thought was unbearable. And anyway, she had married him, and for the last nearly eleven years he'd hated her, and then suddenly, because he'd taken the locum job, they were going to be thrust together and she couldn't understand why he'd agreed.

She hadn't slept all night for thinking about it, and now she was in the crowded staffroom perched on the edge of Lauren's chair with Chloe balanced on the other arm, and all the doctors and reception staff were crowded onto the other seats or clustered round the tea and coffee pots as they waited.

And then Nick strode in, followed by Sam, and she felt his eyes on her instantly.

'Morning, everyone!' Nick said, smiling broadly and rubbing his hands together. 'I'm sorry about the early start, but I wanted to introduce our new locum Sam Cavendish to you. I know some of you will recognise him—Lauren, Chloe, you were probably at school with him—but I'd just like to run through everyone and their jobs, to help you find your feet, Sam. Now, from left to right, Gemma Johnson and Lara Mercer are our practice nurses—Gemma, I know you met many years ago.'

Met? *Met*? Gemma nearly laughed out loud, but the tears were too close to the surface to let go that much. And Nick was still talking.

'Hazel's now our practice manager but I don't know if you've met Sue Gunnell, our head receptionist, then Kate Althorp you remember—she and Chloe are midwives, Rebecca Grey is one of our district nurses, and Lauren, as you know, is our resident physio.

'As for the medical team, we've got Adam Donnelly, who's another local you may remember, Dragan Lovak who's off sick today, Oliver Fawkner, and Gabriel Devereux who's on loan from France and who we've just persuaded to stay. And that's pretty much us. Sam, do you want to introduce yourself?'

The handshaking over, Sam grunted softly and looked around. 'Yeah, hi, everyone,' he said, his voice soft. 'I do know quite a few of you, certainly by sight, and I wish I could say it was good to be back, but you'll all know my mother's had a stroke and that's why I'm here, so I've agreed to fill in for Lucy just until my mother's recovered, and then I'll be going back to my real job, so for those of you who're having heart failure at the thought of a Cavendish having anything to do with your nearest and dearest, relax. I'll be out of here just the moment I can. In the meantime, I'll do what I can to help, so please, just ask.'

It was said with a smile, and it was greeted with a warm ripple of laughter, but it made Gemma's heart ache. Why was he so sure he wasn't welcome, when it was clear to her, looking around at them, that they were all more than happy to have him back in the fold?

Well, almost all. She couldn't count herself in their number, but her reservations were entirely different, and had things not been the way they were, her life, and Sam's, would have been very different too. But at least she had a life, and if he decided to stay, if in the long term his mother's problems were resolved and he was here by choice, then maybe then she might be able talk to him, tell him why—

'Could I just mention something?' Kate Althorp said. 'I know Sam's stepped in, and we're all very grateful because it means the doctors will have less to do and so Nick might not be so crabby all the time…'

They all laughed—even Nick, she noticed—and then she went on, 'It's become apparent, talking to the mums, that losing Lucy—or more specifically losing our only woman doctor—wasn't universally welcomed, because many of them would rather see a woman for some of the problems that they encounter. Now, Sam is only going to be here for a short while if everything with Linda progresses well, and for her sake I hope it does, but I've heard on the grapevine that Polly Carrick is looking for a change of direction and may be looking for a job—some of you may remember her, very quiet, soft-spoken, nice girl. She used to be Polly Searle. Lauren, she's a little younger than you.'

'I remember her,' Sam said. 'She had her nose in a book all the time—we met at a few careers things for wannabe doctors, and I was surprised at that. She was so quiet—tiny little thing. Bit of a mouse, really.'

'That's her. Well, she's a GP now, in London, but as I say, she might be on the move. And, yes, she is my goddaughter, but she's also a wonderful doctor—and a woman, of course. She's a fantastic listener, and I think she'd be brilliant. Just a thought to drop into the mix, if we find ourselves in a position to employ another doctor at any time. And I don't even know at this stage if she'd be interested, but I think we should consider the issue of having a female doctor on staff very seriously.'

Nick straightened, obviously keen to get on. 'Right. Thank you for that, Kate. We'll bear her in mind. OK, if there's nothing else, I'd like to welcome Sam again and I'm sure you'll find that everyone does what they can to make you feel at home. If it helps, I'm sure someone'll take you under their wing for the day to show you the ropes. Gabriel, perhaps, if you wouldn't mind? And now I'm going to sort out the barbeque or we'll all be eating raw sausages tomorrow. You can get me on my mobile if you need me. Kate?'

The meeting broke up, Kate raising her eyebrows and following Nick with a resigned look on her face, and then as Gemma stood, she found herself hard up against a solid and still achingly familiar body.

'Sorry. I was just coming over to talk to you,' Sam murmured, stepping back hastily, but she could hardly hear him for the roaring in her ears and the thundering of her heart.

'That's fine. Sorry. Um—so what did you want?'

'A quiet word?'

Damn. She didn't want a quiet word with Sam. She didn't want any words with him—unless they were words that would take her back into his arms, and she didn't think those words had ever been invented...

'Not now. I've got a clinic.'

He followed her to the door of her room and stood just inside it, his voice low. 'I'm not going to hold you up. I just wanted to say that I know this situation isn't ideal, but I don't want to make things difficult for you and I'll keep out of your way as much as possible. It's not for long, and nobody knows about us, not really, so I'd like to keep it that way. Less complicated all round.'

And God knows, there are enough complications, she thought sadly. 'Sure,' she said, swallowing and wishing he'd leave her alone, and then there was a tap on the door and Gabriel came and rescued her, taking Sam off to his consulting room on the ground floor to shadow him for the day and leaving her in peace to start her clinic.

'Right, I've spoken to Mike Trevellyan and he's going to deliver the meat tomorrow morning, and they're also donating some ice cream and the vending cart for the day. Have you sorted out the rolls and sauces and so on?'

Kate gave a quiet sigh at Nick's typical need to micromanage everything. 'Yes. The supermarket's delivering everything in the morning, and lots of people have volunteered to bring salads and side dishes, so all we have to do is fire up the barbeque and we're done.'

'Excellent. I've got to pick the oil drums up from Ben and Lucy's barn, and we need charcoal. Shall I do that?'

'If you've got time. Your car's bigger than mine. And we need the tables picked up from the church hall, while you're at it. There'll be someone there from three.'

Kate watched Nick as he jotted down a note to himself, and then when he looked up, she said carefully, 'Do you think it's wise, asking Sam to do the locum job?'

Nick looked startled. 'Well, of course it's wise! For God's sake, Kate, if I can't have a bit of faith in the lad, who can? I've known him all his life—'

'It's not Sam I'm worried about, Nick. It's Gemma.'

'Gemma?'

He looked utterly confused, and for the hundredth time Kate wondered how he could be so incredibly obtuse and emotionally inept. 'Yes, Gemma. Well, Sam and Gemma, to be absolutely accurate.'

'What about them?'

She shrugged. 'I just wondered if it would be difficult for them.'

'Difficult? Why on earth should it be difficult? They had a little fling eleven years ago. Why would that make any difference to them now? It's in the past, Kate.'

'Because they're not over it? You can feel the tension coming off them in waves. It may be in the past, but it's far from over, if the look on Gemma's face is anything to go by, and when she's in the room Sam doesn't know where to look. And just because something's in the past doesn't mean it's resolved,' she added pointedly.

He met her eyes then, a flicker of guilt in them. 'Kate, I don't want to talk about this.'

'I know. You never do. But that won't stop Jeremiah being your son, Nick, and one day you're going to have to accept that, because one day I'm going to have to tell him before he finds out from somebody else.'

'Who?' he snapped sharply. 'Who knows?'

'Well, virtually no one—unless you count the tourist who pointed out how alike you are.'

A dull run of colour stained his neck as he turned away. 'I can't deal with this now.'

'You never can, Nick—and I'm beginning to wonder if you ever will until it's thrust on you by circumstance. But you need to know that if Jem ever asks me, I won't lie to him. I *will* tell him the truth. And he'll have a right to know why his own father wouldn't acknowledge him.'

And without another word, she walked out, head held high and her heart pounding. She was sick of it. Sick of beating her head against a brick wall, sick of Nick stonewalling her on the subject, sickened by everything that had happened that summer—the same summer that Sam and Gemma had had their fling that was so obviously not forgotten.

She just hoped that they had more luck resolving it than she'd had.

To Sam's surprise, remarkably few people commented on his presence in Gabriel's surgery. There was a sign up in Reception telling the patients that he'd be covering Lucy for a while, and far from dragging him out into the car park and setting fire to him, they either smiled politely or ignored him.

That was fine. He didn't want or expect a rapturous welcome. He just wanted to do his job, and by eleven he was clawing the walls.

And Gabriel must have realised it, because in the next gap between patients he pushed back his chair after the last patient and smiled at him.

'OK. You don't need me showing you how to do

this. You can take over from me here now so I can go and do my calls, and Oliver's around if you have a problem. I'll be in this afternoon doing a surgery, so if you think of anything else you need to know, just buzz through and ask one of us, and we should get through the list nice and quickly. Which means I can get home and walk the dog in daylight!'

'Lauren mentioned you've got a dog. I'm babysitting my mother's—I'll have to look out for you on the beach.'

'Maybe we can meet up and sniff tails!' he said with a laugh, and stood up. 'Right, I have to get on, I have calls to make and then I need to amuse myself until afternoon surgery. I gather my fiancée is going to see you at one.'

'Yes. Sorry. I didn't mean to disrupt your lunch-time routine—'

'*Sans fait rien*, it's not a problem. You go and let her torture you, and I'll wander into town and find us a sandwich from the shop when I've finished my calls. Tell her I'll see her later.'

He went out, and Sam carried on with his clinic, surprised at how easily it all came back to him. And how much he was enjoying it, although it was all a little cosy and he had no doubt at all that after a few weeks it would drive him absolutely mad.

His last patient had just left when Hazel buzzed through. 'Sam, I've got a gentleman here who needs to be seen this morning, and you're the only doctor left in the surgery. Would you mind awfully taking a look at him?'

'Of course not,' he agreed, sighed quietly and wondering if he'd find time for lunch before he saw Lauren. Breakfast seemed to have passed him by and he was getting very hungry. Maybe there'd be a biscuit or two left in the staffroom.

There was a tap on the door, and a man in late middle age came in and sat down.

'Hello, Sam.'

He frowned. There was a not-too-distant memory of some washing tied to the top of a tree, and he gave an inward groan. 'Mr Reynolds.'

'I see you haven't forgotten me, then?'

'Indeed not. Apparently it's mutual.' He gave a slight smile, and Mr Reynolds smiled back.

'I didn't expect to see you back here. I'm sorry about your mother.'

'Thank you,' he said for what must have been the hundredth time since he'd come back. 'So what can I do for you today, Mr Reynolds?'

'It's my angina. I just can't seem to get on top of it today, and I've been puffing away on the old GTN and—well, I don't know, it doesn't seem to be making any difference.'

'Just slip your jacket off, let's check your blood pressure,' Sam said. 'Have you been overdoing it?'

'I did a bit of gardening this morning, but I don't know if it was a good idea.'

'Well, your blood pressure's a little high, and I can see you're on medication for it, and you're on a statin. Can you describe your symptoms?' he asked as he took off the cuff and made a note of the reading. And what he heard, he didn't like at all.

'OK, I think just to be on the safe side I'm going to give you a little aspirin—you don't have asthma, do you? No? OK, just chew this up and we'll get a nurse to run an ECG on you—no, stay there, don't get up.

I'll go and find someone. I just want to make sure nothing's going on.'

He left the door open and asked Hazel if there was a nurse free, just as Gemma came downstairs. 'Do you want something done?' she asked, and he nodded.

'Please. An ECG for Mr Reynolds. His angina's bothering him.'

He lifted a brow, and Gemma nodded her understanding of the urgency. 'I'll get the ECG machine. His angina's a bit unstable.'

She came into his room wheeling the machine a few moments later, just as Sam had settled Mr Reynolds on the couch.

'Hello, Ron, what've you been up to? I bet you've been gardening, haven't you?' she asked, peeling the backing off the electrodes and sticking them on Mr Reynolds's hairy chest.

'How did you guess?'

She smiled, and Sam's heart turned over. No wonder Mr Reynolds's angina was unstable! 'Ah, well, a little bird told me the family were coming for the weekend. I hope you're all coming to the barbeque tomorrow.'

'Wouldn't miss it, Gemma. Never have.'

'Excellent. Right, just lie still while I run the printout, and while I've got you there, I'm going to give you a little lecture about your diet, because I can see from your tummy that you've been down to the chippy a few times too many, haven't you?'

'Nothing gets by you, does it?' he said with a little smile, and Gemma chuckled.

'Not much, not in this village. And anyway, I saw you and Doreen sitting on the harbour wall eating them last Saturday. So it'll be low-fat sausages for you at the barbeque tomorrow. I'll get Dr Tremayne to buy some specially.'

But just then the ECG trace began to flutter, and he pressed his hand to his chest and groaned.

'Well, that'll save worrying about the low-fat sausages,' Sam murmured in her ear, and she stepped aside, raising the backrest as Sam took over and sat their patient up to ease the load on his heart. 'I think you might be having a little heart attack, Ron, so I'm going to send you off to St Piran's to get checked out.'

'Are you sure? You do know what you're doing, don't you?' he said with a wry grin. 'Only I wouldn't have wanted you to miss the lecture on heart attacks—Aaah!'

'Just sit back and try to relax, and I'll give you some painkillers. That should make it a bit easier. Gemma, could you ask Hazel to call the ambulance and his wife and then draw me up some diamorphine—ten milligrams, I think. Thank you. And you just lie there and thank your lucky stars I attended that lecture, Ron, and don't you worry about a thing. It's all under control.'

And less than fifteen minutes later he was off to hospital, and Sam left Gemma tidying up the ECG machine.

'Right, I'm sorry, I'll have to leave you to it, I'm supposed to be seeing Lauren at one and I'm already late,' he said, and with a resigned sigh Sam crossed the wide corridor and tapped on Lauren's door.

It opened instantly, and she came out with a smile. 'Hi, Sam. Come on in.'

He shut the door, then hesitated. Did he strip off to his boxers, or wait for her to take a history? 'I'm sorry I'm late, I got held up with a patient.'

'Don't worry. Just peel your things off behind the screen and I'll take a history as we go along. Maybe I'd better have a look at all your injuries today, and we can sort out a treatment plan.'

'Well, good luck with that,' he said with a dry chuckle, and dropped into the chair behind the screen while he took off his shoes and socks and unbuttoned his shirt. He really, really didn't want to do this, but if he ignored the problem it would get worse, and he couldn't expect to make progress if he neglected his physio. No gain without pain and all that, but he'd frankly had it with the pain and it was growing old very quickly.

'OK, let's go through this from the top because we've got no notes on you, of course. So—what exactly happened?'

'Oh, no.'

She picked up the specs off the desk and hefted them in her hand. Sam was bound to be going in to visit his mother later, and he'd just popped in for a chat with Lauren, presumably about another patient. She'd give them to him, he'd be able to take them to Mr Reynolds.

And then she'd go for a walk along the harbour, maybe pick something up to eat on the way. Anything rather than sitting around in the staffroom and waiting for Sam to come in, and as long as they were both in the building, she'd be on edge.

She tapped on Lauren's door and stuck her head round without waiting for a reply, knowing that Lauren was free because Gabriel was out and her patients had all gone, but to her horror she wasn't free. Not free at all, and the patient lying propped up her couch, wearing nothing but snug jersey boxers, was Sam.

'Well, come in,' he said drily, and she felt hot colour scorch her cheeks.

'I'm sorry, I didn't realize…' She trailed off, her eyes taking in the still-purple scars that slashed across his chest and shoulder, then sucked in a breath as she saw his leg. The skin must have been torn as he'd slid along the ground, because the outside of his left thigh was a mess. He'd had skin grafts, but they could never cover it completely, she knew that. It would always leave a nasty, disfiguring scar. And lower down, on his shin, were the marks of an external fixator, and on the outside of his ankle further evidence of surgery.

Dear God. He must have been through hell—was still going through it, if the faint sheen of sweat on his skin was anything to go by, and Lauren was standing there holding his foot in her hand and quietly waiting for Gemma to free herself from her trance and either say her piece or leave.

'Sorry, I'll—I just wanted to give you these. Mr Reynolds's specs. I thought you could drop them into him at the hospital while you're visiting Linda,' she croaked, and, dumping them on the desk, she fled out of the room and ran out of the building, all thoughts of lunch forgotten, driven out by the image burned on her mind—the image of Sam, so severely wounded yet so dismissive of his injuries that she'd had no *idea* they had been so bad, or that he must have come so very, very close to death…

She crossed the road and sat on the harbour wall, her shaking arms wrapped round her waist as she stared out over the muddy harbour where the fishing boats were stranded by the low tide, and tried to see something other than that image of his broken, damaged body on Lauren's couch.

And all the time she'd been staring at him, she realised, he'd been smiling a wry, bitter, twisted little smile that tore her heart in two.

Something wet landed on her arm, and she looked down. Another drop landed, and this time she'd felt it sliding down her cheek.

Stupid. So, so stupid. He didn't want to know her. He'd promised to keep out of her way, had said he wanted to keep their relationship quiet. He sure as hell didn't want her tears.

But still they fell, as fast as she could swipe them away, and in the end she got off the wall and ran down beyond the lifeboat station to the rocks on the headland and sat hugging her knees until the shock had receded and she felt she'd regained her composure enough to go back to the surgery and face him.

Then, and only then, did she stand up and turn round—and saw Sam, just a few feet away, perched on a rock and watching her with guarded eyes.

'I'm so sorry I barged in,' she began, but he just arched a brow.

'You need to learn to wait when you knock.'

'I know. Believe me, I wish I had.'

'What—too shocking for you, was it? A little bit too real?'

She felt sick. 'Sam, don't be horrible. You know it's not that.'

'Do I? I'm not sure what I know any more. And why the hell are you so upset? You walked away, Gemma. You didn't want me then—so what's changed enough now to make you cry?'

Nothing. Nothing had changed. She'd always loved him—always wanted him, always missed him. And that was why she'd left him, why she'd gone away and done what she'd had to do alone, so that if the worst came to the worst, he could move on with his life without her.

Except he hadn't, apparently. Like her, he'd been in limbo. And like her, he'd almost died.

She held his eyes. 'Nothing's changed, Sam. It was just the shock—I didn't realise you'd been so badly injured. The other night, you gave me no idea it had been so bad.'

He shrugged. 'It was just one of those things. You get on with it, don't you? I mean, you can't change it, so what's the point of bleating about it?'

He walked slowly up to her, moving carefully over the rocks, and lifting his right hand he brushed away the tears that still stained her cheeks. Apart from the one tear the other night in the Smugglers', he'd only ever seen her cry right at the end, when her parents had found out they were married and had said terrible, cruel things to her. And he hated to see her like this.

'Don't cry for me,' he said gruffly. 'I'm all right, Gemma. It's over now, there's no need to cry. I don't need your pity, I'm fine.'

But the tears were still leaking slowly from her eyes, welling up and sliding down her cheeks, glistening in the sunshine, and he couldn't help himself. He tried to stop, tried to hold himself back, but somehow his lips were there, on her cheek, kissing away the tears.

And then not just the tears. His mouth found hers, just lightly brushing it, their breath mingling as they took tiny, shallow gasps of air, little shuddering breaths as they slowly, tenderly explored the soft flesh they'd both ached for for so long.

But it wasn't enough. It could never be enough, and when a tiny, frantic little whimper escaped her, it was too much for him. With a ragged groan he threaded his fingers through her hair and took her mouth in a kiss so wild, so needy, so desperate that when he lifted his head long moments later it was like tearing away part of his soul.

'Sam?'

Her voice was trembling, her body quivering against him, and he forced himself to take a step back, to distance himself from the one person in the world who could still hurt him.

'No, Gemma. I'm not going there again. I can't.'

'I didn't ask you to.'

'But I want to,' he said, the words dragged from him. 'How can I want to? You walked away from me—you just walked away—why?'

She felt pain close like a fist around her heart, wishing she could tell him the truth but not really knowing how, not now, after all this time. 'We were kids, Sam. It was a long time ago. And maybe it was wrong. Maybe I shouldn't have gone, but at the time I felt I had no choice. My life was—it was going in a direction I hadn't planned, and I didn't know what to do. And I made a mistake.'

'So—what are you saying, Gemma? You want to try again?'

'No. Yes. I don't know,' she said tearfully, not wanting it to be like this, so very different from what she might have planned. 'I really don't know what I want, and I certainly don't know you, not now. Maybe I never did. Maybe you never knew me. Maybe we need to find out who we are now, what we're looking for—because we haven't moved on, either of us, have we? Not really.'

He stared at her, his eyes shielded again, although she could see the emotions on his face from the set of his lips and the slight flicker of a muscle in his jaw.

'I don't know,' he said at last, his voice taut. 'I'm not sure I can do this. I don't want to talk about it, and I haven't got time for it. I've got other priorities now. I've got to go and do a surgery, and then I have to take Jamie to see my mother. He still hasn't been.'

'Maybe he's frightened she'll die? Or that she'll lean on him, and he's afraid he can't cope? Sound familiar, Sam?'

His laugh was bitter. 'Yeah, but she won't lean on him. She'll lean on me, like she's always done, because that's my job, isn't it? I'm the man of the house, the head of the family. And I don't need it any more than I need this all raking up again. So forgive me if I don't feel like exploring my emotions with you to see if you made a mistake or if you really did mean it when you walked out on us. I've got enough on my plate. You made your bed, Gemma. Go and lie in it.'

And turning on his heel, he walked away and left her there, her slender hope for their future happiness in tatters.

'Mummy! Mummy, can we have Matt to stay tonight? Please please *please*!'

Kate smiled ruefully down at her son, hanging on her arm and begging, while those dark brown eyes so very like his father's implored her to say yes. 'Darling, we can't tonight, I'm sorry, because I've got the barbeque to set up in the morning with Uncle Nick, but maybe tomorrow night?'

'Could I offer to have Jem instead?'

She looked up into the man's kind, straightforward

face and wondered about him. He was a teacher at the senior school, a widower, apparently, and his son Matthew Werrick was one of Jem's friends, but so far she'd never really had anything to do with him.

He held out his hand. 'We haven't been properly introduced. I'm Rob.'

She smiled and took his hand, warm, firm and uncomplicated. She had a feeling it matched its owner. 'I'm Kate. It's nice to meet you—and I'm sorry about Jem. He's been asking for ages about Matthew coming to stay, but tonight's really not good. Maybe another time.'

'I can have them tonight. I'm more than happy to.'

'Oh, we wouldn't dream of imposing, Rob.'

'It's not an imposition at all. Actually it would be fun. The weekends can get a bit long, can't they?'

Oh, yes. And the children were begging. Yet still she hesitated, and his mouth curved into an understanding smile.

'Don't worry about it, Kate. You don't know me. That's reasonable, but perhaps instead of the night, why don't you drop him off in the morning on your way to the barbeque, and I can bring them both down later and meet you there? We were planning on coming, anyway. Would that be better?'

'Oh, Mummy, I want to go to Matthew's for the night! Please, please!'

'Jeremiah, don't, that's rude,' she chided, but Matthew was pleading with his father, and Rob gave her a 'suit yourself' shrug and a smile, and she gave in.

'If you really don't mind, I'm quite happy for him to stay with you. And it's nothing to do with not knowing you, it's more that I have problems returning favours because of work.'

'Well, I don't think we need to worry about that, do we?' he said with an understanding and good-humoured smile. 'I'm more than happy to have Matthew's friends over. So—do you want to collect his things and drop him round to me? Or come with him at six and I'll feed you both. Rumour has it I can manage to hurl together a half decent Bolognese sauce—so if you'd like…?'

Actually, yes, she realised suddenly, she *would* like. She'd spent the last thirty years waiting for Nick to notice her, and the only time he had, it had been devastating. She hadn't been on a date since she'd started going out with James, and it was nearly eleven years since he'd died. And apart from James, there had only been that one time with Nick, on the night of the storm, the night James had died…

So, yes, she would like. And although it was only a simple supper invitation, for Kate it was a quantum leap. So drawing in a breath, she smiled at Rob and threw herself into the void.

CHAPTER FOUR

'I'M NOT coming.'

Sam propped himself up against the worktop and folded his arms. 'Why are you scared, Jamie? Is it because you don't know what to expect?'

'I'm not scared.'

Sam sighed. 'Of course you are. Your mother's had a stroke, and people die of them. Every day. So, sure you're scared. It's only reasonable. Dammit, I'm scared.' Scared he'd end up trapped here, scared he'd never get away again and he'd be stuck with Gemma in the same town, bumping into each other and driving him insane with wanting.

'Is she going to die?'

'Well, of course she is, we all are, but not now. At least, I don't believe so, anyway. They think she's got an underlying heart condition—nothing serious, just an irregular beat that could cause her blood to clot, and if that's the case, she'll have anticoagulant drugs to slow her clotting and antiarrhythmics to make her heart beat evenly.'

'What, to go with the blood-pressure drugs and the anti-depressants?' he said lightly, but Sam could tell there was real fear there lurking underneath his flip remark, and he wished he knew him well enough, wished he was close enough to his brother to pull him into his arms and hug him.

Wished there'd been anyone there to do it to him, when his father had walked out and left him—literally—holding the baby.

But there hadn't, and Jamie wouldn't let him anyway, so instead he opened the fridge, poured two glasses of juice and pushed one towards Jamie across the kitchen table. 'She'll be all right, Jamie. She's already so much better.'

'It's my fault.'

'No, of course it's not your fault. It's her fault. She's never looked after herself properly.'

'No. It's my fault. We had a row. I got really angry with her, and we were yelling, and I went out. And I didn't come back until after midnight. And if Gemma hadn't found her…'

'She would have died?' he said softly. 'Maybe. But that's not your fault. Lots of people have rows. It doesn't kill them.'

'It nearly killed Mum.'

'No. The stroke nearly killed her. You didn't. And she misses you. I think she wants to make up.'

'Did she say so?'

He shook his head. 'No. But she's very keen to see you.'

Jamie sat there for a moment, then drained the glass and stood up. 'So what are we waiting for?' he asked, and headed for the door.

'Hi, Mum.'

'Jamie! You came!' his mother said, and, holding out her arms, she wrapped her youngest son against her heart, and Sam swallowed the lump in his throat and turned away.

And there, catching him with his emotional trousers down, was Gemma, carrying a vase of flowers. 'Hi. You got him here, then,' she said softly, and he nodded.

'Yeah. Thanks.'

'Thanks?'

'It was what you said, about him being scared. They'd had a row and he thought it was all his fault. Look, are you done here? I was thinking—maybe we could go and get a coffee?'

'So you can salve your conscience about being nasty to me at lunchtime?' she said, her eyes reproachful. 'I don't think so, Sam. And, yes, I am done,' she added pointedly. 'I'm going home—to lie in my bed.'

She put the flowers down on the locker and dropped a kiss on Linda's cheek. 'You take care, and I'll see you when you get home. Bye, Jamie. Nice to see you again.'

And she walked out of the ward, her back straight and her head held high.

His words echoed back at him, and he felt a wash of guilt. Damn. He gave his mother what had to be an awkward smile. 'I'm just going to go and get a coffee. I'll leave you two alone for a minute, you've got a lot of catching up to do and I missed lunch. I won't be long.'

She smiled knowingly, and Jamie just grinned, and he ground his teeth and followed Gemma out.

'Gemma? Please, wait.'

She stopped and waited, but her face was expressionless. 'What?'

'Just—I'm sorry. I didn't— Look, this isn't easy.'

'Tell me about it,' she muttered.

'Please. Come and have a coffee with me. Give me a chance to apologise.'

She looked up into his eyes, saw the signs of strain around them, and because she loved him—had always loved him, ever since the first time she'd seen him walking on the beach twelve years ago, a boy on the brink of manhood—she nodded. 'OK. But you're buying.'

They found a canteen that was open, and he ordered two lattes, picked a couple of sandwiches out of the fridge at random and paid for them, then followed Gemma to a table.

'Tuna and cucumber or roast beef and horseradish?'

'Chicken salad,' she said, taking the tuna, and smiled, and saw the tension drain out of him.

'They're going to give me hell for this. Mum gave me such a knowing look, and Jamie was grinning. I should have let you get further ahead before I came out after you,' he grumbled, struggling to open the other packet of sandwiches.

She watched discreetly, noting that he was obviously finding his finger and thumb uncooperative and the lack of feedback was hampering him. She concentrated on unwrapping her own sandwich and munching into it, and after a moment he succeeded, and she was able to relax.

'Your mother seems quite keen to get us back together again,' she said conversationally, and he stopped, his sandwich halfway to his open mouth.

'What's she said now?'

She shrugged. 'Just asked how things were going at work. I didn't tell her.'

He felt his neck heat. 'That was—I was just—'

'Defensive? I'm a nurse, Sam. I've seen worse.'

But not on him, and it had shocked her much more than she would have believed possible. She took another bite of her sandwich to give her mouth something to do, but even so the silence stretched out until Sam broke it, his voice taut and strangely impassive.

'She kept telling me that you asked after me. In her letters. Why did you do that?'

Because I love you? Because I needed to know— anything, any scrap of information, anything to keep my love alive...

'Well, I have to talk about something during a consultation,' she said lightly, 'and you're as good a topic as any.'

And the only one of any interest to her, but he didn't have to know that.

'So it wasn't that you wanted to know?'

Oh, lord, she couldn't do this. She put her sandwich down and met his eyes. 'Sam, of course I wanted to know how you were doing,' she said, giving up the pretence. 'It's not as if I hate you.'

'But you don't love me. You didn't—not enough to stay.'

Or too much...

'Sam, we were so young.'

'I *loved* you,' he said roughly, throwing down his sandwich and leaning forwards, his eyes glittering. 'I really, really loved you, Gemma—and you just walked away. And you didn't even tell me to my face. That was the thing that hurt most—that you couldn't even talk to me. After all we'd shared—'

He broke off, sat back and shook his head.

'This was a lousy idea. I can't do it, Gemma. I'm sorry. It would be too easy to let myself get sucked back in, but I've been hurt too damned much by you, and I'm not letting it happen again.'

And without another glance at her, he got to his feet and walked away from her, leaving her in a litter of unwanted sandwiches and half-finished coffee and broken promises.

The barbeque was in full swing when he walked down there the following afternoon, and the first person to greet him was Lucy.

'Sam? Oh, Sam, it's so *good* to see you!' she cried. Handing a tiny baby over to the man at her side, she threw herself into his arms and hugged him. Then she let him go, stood back and stared at him, laughing and shaking her head in disbelief.

'Goodness, you have got *so* damned good-looking! I can just hear the clatter of the locks with everyone shutting their daughters up! Come, I want you to meet Ben and the children.'

And she dragged him over to the man he assumed was Ben, and took the baby back out of his arms. 'This is Ben Carter, my husband, and the little tyke round his neck is Annabel, and this is Josh. Guys, this is Sam Cavendish. He taught me how to light fires and climb trees and—'

'I'm not sure I want to know what he taught you,' Ben said with a dry chuckle, but his handshake was friendly enough and Sam could see the bone-deep confidence in their relationship that shone from both of them.

And he envied it. God, how he envied it. To have a love that profound and know it was returned...

'Gemma's here,' Lucy said softly, her eyes concerned.

'I know.' Of course he knew. His radar had clocked her the moment he walked into the surgery car park which turned annually into the site for the Penhally Bay Independent Lifeboat Association fundraiser. She would be here, he'd known that. Maybe in a perverse way it was even why he'd come, unable to stay away. Even after yesterday, after all that had been said, after two failed attempts at building bridges, he couldn't stay away.

But Lucy was one of the few people in Penhally who knew the whole story, and he knew he could rely on her to keep her thoughts to herself.

'Dad tells me you're working at the practice. That must make things a bit interesting,' she murmured.

'It's fine,' he said, trying not to think about just how fine it wasn't.

'That's what Dad said, but I didn't believe him, any more than I believe you. So—how's your mother? That was a bit of a shocker.'

'She's OK. She's coming home on Tuesday.'

'Oh. Right. Will you be OK to work?'

'Yes. I have to be, I can't sit and look at her all day, and anyway she's made fantastic progress. The new specialist stroke unit's brilliant. And if she needs it, she'll have physio and occupational therapy and maybe even someone from the community psychiatric team to make sure she's coping with the changes in her life. And she'll need to rest and get her confidence back slowly, and I'm only going to be working part time.'

Ben laughed at that. 'That's what Lucy said—but somehow, if you aren't careful, the part time grows. There's the odd clinic here and the occasional surgery there, and before you know where you are the only thing missing is the on-call.'

'Well, it's all a change from working all day and being on call all night seven days a week in a shanty town or some isolated clinic in the bush. And having drugs on tap is a revelation, as is being able to drive down the road without wondering if you're about to be ambushed or blown up.'

A frown crossed Lucy's face. 'Yes, Dad mentioned that. How are you now?'

He smiled. 'I'm fine,' he said, his stock reply, and really, he supposed, he was, if you didn't count the scars and the horrified look on Gemma's face. And he was enjoying being back at work, just as he was enjoying seeing Lucy again, and meeting her husband and her babies, and being there at the barbeque. Tame and bucolic and very, very English, he thought drily, but somehow safe.

And if it wasn't for Gemma threatening his peace of mind, he might almost be tempted…

Nick turned the sausages on the barbeque while he smiled mechanically at the busy throng and wondered if Kate was right about Sam and Gemma. They'd been avoiding each other—not hard, in the crowd, but it seemed odd that Gemma hadn't gone up to Lucy and said hello, and he wondered if that was because Sam was there talking to Ben and cuddling the baby. And ignoring Gemma, in turn?

Possibly. Frankly, he had no idea, and he wondered if that should worry him. Was he really so blind to people's emotions as Kate implied?

Or was it just that his own life was so filled with pain that he'd shut himself down?

Take the business of Jeremiah—

'Mummy, we're here! Hi, Uncle Nick. We're starving. Can Matt and me have a burger please, Mum?'

'I should think so, love,' Kate said, smiling indulgently at him across the barbeque while Nick stood poised with the tongs and stared at the boy who was his son, and then she lifted her eyes and smiled at the man with the children. Robert Werrick, Nick realised, and felt a prickle of something that felt uncomfortably like—jealousy?

Ridiculous! Of course it wasn't! But her greeting to Werrick then made it obvious that the boys had spent the night at his house and been with him for the day, and he suddenly wondered if—

No. Of course she wasn't seeing him! And, anyway, it was none of his business if she was. But it didn't stop it feeling just a little bit odd, and not altogether pleasant...

Gemma spent the rest of the bank holiday weekend blitzing her house.

Her parents had bought Seagull Cottage with the express intention of having somewhere convenient, easy to maintain and with a lovely setting, and all of those things made it ideal for Gemma, so when she'd moved back, she'd persuaded her parents to let her rent it from them.

And it had been perfect.

The garden was just a paved area with pots standing around on it and enough room for a little table and chairs, and because of the mild climate many of the things in the pots over-wintered, so it was just a case of tidying up from time to time. No grass, no hedges, no weeding—but that weekend, frankly, she could have done with all of them, just to keep her a little bit busier and take her mind off Sam.

She would have gone to St Piran's and visited Linda, but she knew Sam's sisters would be there over the weekend and, besides, so would he. There would be plenty of time to visit her once she was home, and she could choose a time when Sam was out. So with nothing better to do and the garden tidied within an inch of its life, she spring-cleaned the house.

Completely.

She turned out her bedroom, changed the sheets, wiped down the woodwork, polished the furniture—she even wiped the bulbs in the light fittings—and then she did the same to the other two rooms and the bathroom before moving downstairs and blitzing the living area.

She even cleaned out the fridge, her least favourite job in the world, and by the end of Monday the washing was done, there was a pile of ironing she could scarcely see over and she was exhausted.

So exhausted that when she went into work on Tuesday morning, having girded her loins for bumping into Sam, she'd completely forgotten that Linda was being discharged and he wouldn't be in.

And the disappointment was extraordinary.

Oh, well. She threw herself into her work—mostly baby inoculations with some travel vaccinations for people planning their summer breaks, and then she went upstairs to the staffroom to make herself a drink and found Lauren there.

Damn.

'Hi, there. Can I make you another drink?' she asked cheerfully, but Lauren wasn't fooled. Not that she said anything, just shook her head and asked how Linda was, but the jump from Gemma's 'Do you want a drink' to Lauren's 'How's Linda' was pretty darned remote—

unless your mind was already there, Gemma thought with resignation.

'She's fine, I think. Doing really well, but you can tell me more once you've treated her. I take it you're going to be doing her physio?'

'I expect so. Are you going to hand her over to Rebecca for her continuing care, or are you going to pop in on your way home so you can give her more continuity?'

And see Sam. 'I'll see how she is, I think,' Gemma said, trying hard to sound casual. 'If she's relatively stable, there won't be much to do apart from regular INR checks for her anticoagulants, so Sam could take the bloods and bring them in. In fact, he could do all of it. He's only here part time.'

'So you don't have to go there?' Lauren said softly, and Gemma looked up swiftly and met her concerned eyes, teabag poised on the spoon, and then she turned back and threw the teabag in the bin, put milk in her tea and sat down.

'Why wouldn't I want to go there?' she asked, and Lauren sighed gently.

'OK, you don't have to tell me, but if you need someone to talk to—I know Sam had a thing for you all those years ago.'

'A thing?' she said, trying to sound puzzled, but Lauren wasn't stupid and she gave her friend a patient look.

'The girls in his year were gutted, so it was hardly a secret, Gemma. And I saw your face on Friday. You were devastated when you saw his injuries, and if you ask me he was pretty devastated that you'd seen them. He wasn't going to come after you, but then he asked my advice.'

'And you told him to follow me?'

'No. I told him to follow his heart. And then I was

upstairs getting something from the treatment room and
I saw him kiss you.'

'That would have been right before he told me I'd
made my bed and I should lie on it,' she said with a trace
of bitterness, and Lauren sucked in her breath and
reached out a hand.

'Gemma, I'm so sorry. It must be so difficult for
you, working with him. Why on earth did he agree?'

She shrugged. 'I have no idea. Because Nick's very
persuasive? Because he genuinely thought it would be
all right?'

'Or because he thought it would give you a chance
to get to know each other again in a way that gives you
both an opportunity to retreat without loss of face?'

She thought about that for a moment, but it didn't
seem to feel right. 'I don't think so. I don't think it was
that premeditated. And he didn't look any more pleased
than I felt, to be honest, so, no, I don't think it was that,
but I can't for the life of me work out why—especially
as Linda's making such amazing progress. By Friday
night, you'd hardly know she'd had a stroke on Tuesday.
It's incredible.'

'I know. I've seen other people who've been treated
there, and it's fantastic what that rapid intervention with
clot-busters does,' Lauren agreed, and to Gemma's
relief the subject moved away from Linda—and, more
specifically, from her elder son.

But only for now. She knew perfectly well that
Lauren would be watching, and because she'd be
treating Sam, too, and because patients having physical
therapy often talked quite revealingly to their therapist,
Lauren would probably hear more than Gemma wanted
her to.

But it would be safe with her. Her friend wasn't a gossip and, apart from her professionalism, she was the soul of kindness. She'd look after Sam, support and encourage him, and give him the help he needed to get his life back on track.

And if that meant that in the end he left Penhally again to return to Africa, Gemma would just have to accept it…

CHAPTER FIVE

'JAMIE! Get up! You've got to be at school in twenty minutes, and I need to get Mum up and dressed before I go to work in half an hour, so I haven't got time to drive you!'

'For God's sake, bro, chill! I'll be fine.'

'No, you'll be late,' Sam said, stripping off the quilt and hoisting Jamie out of bed one-handed. 'Now get washed and dressed and get to school before you get suspended.'

'I should be so lucky,' he mumbled, but Sam wasn't going to pick that one up in this lifetime, so he went downstairs and found his mother tangled in her bra.

'Oh, Mum, let me help you with that,' he said gently, and sorted her out, getting the straps in the right place and then hugging her as the tears of frustration filled her eyes. 'Come on, you're doing so well.'

'It's just all so unnecessary! If only it hadn't happened...'

'I know. But it did, and luckily Gemma was here.'

She put a hand on his arm. 'Sam, don't hurt her.'

He stared at his mother in astonishment. 'Me, hurt Gemma? Mum, she walked out on me!'

'But she loves you, Sam. It's so obvious.'

'Not to me, it isn't.'

'Well, then, you're blind, and you probably don't deserve her. Come on, help me into that top and then you'd better go or you'll be late for work.'

He waited until she was settled in her favourite chair opposite the window with a view over the harbour, and then he paused.

'Are you sure you'll be all right?' he asked, still torn about leaving her, but she just smiled sadly.

'I'll have to be, Sam—and you're not exactly far away. And I've got the phone and all I have to do is press 1 and I'll get the surgery, so I'll be fine, and I've got Digger for company. Go on—and take Jamie to school or he'll be bunking off again.'

'For heaven's sake, he should just—'

'Please, Sam. He's in enough trouble.'

'OK, I'll take him. There are drinks in the fridge, and I'll leave the back door unlocked so Lauren can get in. And don't boil the kettle!'

'No, darling,' she said with a long-suffering smile, and he kissed her cheek, grabbed his keys, yelled for Jamie and started the car.

'Linda?'

'Gemma? Hello, sweetheart. How kind of you to drop in.'

'Not at all, it's always a pleasure to see you. I'm parched. Do you fancy a cup of tea?'

'Oh, I'd love one! Sam won't let me near the kettle at the moment, and I know fruit juice and water are good for you, but, oh, I do miss my tea!'

'You'll be telling me in a minute that he's hidden

all your chocolate,' Gemma teased, and Linda rolled her eyes.

'Don't. Don't even go there. He rations it. I don't know where he keeps it, but I'm allowed one square a day, apparently. Too much saturated fat. And it has to be the dark stuff, like you said, or he won't let me have it at all. He's a tyrant.'

'But you love him.'

'And I'm not alone, am I?' she said softly, and Gemma nearly dropped the teapot.

'Linda, really—I don't think—'

'Don't panic. He doesn't see it, but if he'd only give you both a chance…'

'Linda, he doesn't like me.'

'Sam? Of course he likes you. He's just wary. Now, I don't know what went on between you two, and it's not my business, but he hasn't been the same since you left. He's like he was after his father went—defiant and defensive, but I thought he'd get over it—get over you, but he doesn't seem to have done. So—don't give up, Gemma. Please, don't give up. Not without trying.'

'Don't give up what?'

'Sam!'

This time she did drop the pot. It slipped through her fingers and hit the worktop, and only Sam's hand flying out to steady it prevented an accident.

'Guilty conscience?' he murmured, and she turned and glared at him.

'Not at all! You frightened the life out of me, sneaking up behind me like that!'

'Sneaking? It's my house! I'm allowed to walk in—and I didn't sneak. I'm just not noisy.'

'I didn't hear your car.'

'That's because I could see yours here, so I left it at work and walked home in case there wasn't room on the drive. I'll go and pick it up later—take the dog out for a run. So is there tea in that pot, or are you just posing for effect?'

She nearly threw it at him.

'Ron Reynolds is home.'

Sam was lounging in the doorway to her room the following afternoon, and Gemma looked up from her notes.

'Is he? Good. How's he doing?'

'OK. It was an MI, so he's another one on anticoagulants for your INR checks. They've done a balloon angioplasty apparently and he's much improved. He'll need checking on, but he should be all right to come here to your clinic.'

'Well, if not I'll ask Rebecca to do it. So how come he knew you? Because it sounds as though he did, quite well.'

Sam's face was wry. 'Oh, he did. He lived quite near us, and I guess he had quite a lot to put up with. I took their washing off the line one night and hung it in the top of the fir tree in the front garden. It wouldn't have been so bad if it hadn't been for his daughter's underwear. She was a bit of a goer, Amy Reynolds, and her underwear was a legend.'

Gemma laughed. 'And were you familiar with the underwear before this occasion?'

He chuckled. 'Sadly not—well, only from the washing line. We could see it from the top of the tree in the Tremaynes' back garden next door. Jack, Ed and I used to go up there and try and spy on her through her bedroom window.'

'Sam!'

'What? We were about fourteen! We were just kids, Gemma. We didn't know anything about sex then, really. It was just a bit of harmless fun.'

'You weren't so harmless when you were nineteen,' she said rashly, and then could have bitten her tongue as he went still.

'No. But that was different, Gemz. You were my wife.'

Gemz. He'd only ever called her that when they were alone. She looked away, her mind flooded with memories. Intimate memories, of the time they'd spent together. His touch, his soft, coaxing voice, his gentleness—his passion, finally unleashed and exquisitely shocking in its awesome power to thrill her. She swallowed hard. 'Sam, I—'

'It's all right,' he said softly. 'It's in the past, Gemma. Let's just leave it there. I have to get on. I'll see you.'

And shrugging away from the doorpost, he crossed the landing and went down the stairs, and she listened to his limp and wanted to cry for everything they'd lost and the fact that there just didn't seem to be any way back.

Damn.

He couldn't concentrate. He couldn't think about anything other than Gemma, about how she'd felt in his arms, how much fun they'd had, the laughter they'd shared, and how it had felt to hold her long into the night, just talking about anything and everything.

He couldn't remember anything they'd not been able to talk about, and yet now—now every conversation seemed to lead back to them, and the fact that they'd split up, and it was like a minefield. And he knew, from bitter personal experience, just how dangerous *they* could be.

But he couldn't stay away from her, couldn't ignore her. Couldn't, despite his best efforts, manage to keep away. And at the bottom of his heart, hidden low down behind all the disillusion and pain, was a gut feeling that there was something going on, something he hadn't known about—something she was keeping from him. So maybe she was right. Maybe what they needed to do was try again, see if they could make a go of it this time—and maybe now she'd trust him enough to share whatever it was that had taken her away from him.

No. He felt himself recoiling from the idea, curiously unwilling to disturb the status quo, the unstable truce they seemed to have established. Perhaps to try and pick up their relationship where they'd left off was too much, too soon—but what if they wound the clock back further, maybe, to when they'd met? Pretended they'd just met now, that they were strangers and they were attracted to each other and they were just starting out?

Would it work? Give them a chance to get to know the people they were now, and see if there was any way forward from there?

He didn't know, but he was going to give it a damn good try, because his time back in Penhally had proved to him, above all else, that he couldn't live without her. Not live. He could exist, as he'd been existing for the last eleven years. But live? No. Not without his beloved Gemz.

So he'd suggest they start from scratch, as if they'd just met. Strangers. It could be interesting. Fun. And maybe...

All he had to do was talk her into it. Whistling softly, he left his consulting room and ran upstairs and tapped on her door, but it was opened by Lara Mercer, the other practice nurse.

'Ah. Is Gemma here, Lara?'

'No, sorry Sam, she's gone home. She said something about dropping in on your mother on the way, but that was half an hour ago.'

'Right. OK, thanks.'

'Is there a message?'

'No. No message.' At least, not one he'd leave with anyone.

He drove home, wondering if she'd still be there, and she was, so he pulled in behind her—to stop her getting away? Maybe. Then he went inside, calling as he did to avoid the possibility of her accusing him of sneaking up on her.

She was just leaving, picking up her bag and keys, and he wondered if she'd seen his car pull up and decided to get out of his way. He couldn't blame her if she did, because every encounter seemed to peel another layer off their defences.

'Could you move your car for me, Sam?' she asked, not quite looking at him, but he wasn't ready to let her go.

'Can we have a chat first?'

She looked at him, searching his face for clues. 'What about?'

He gave a crooked, slightly uncertain smile that tipped her heart off kilter. 'Oh, this and that. Can we take the dog and go up to the headland? He could do with a little run.'

She hesitated, but then Linda came out into the kitchen and kissed Sam on the cheek. 'Hello, darling. I'm just going to have a lie-down for a few minutes. It's been a long day. Call me when you get back from your walk.'

So there was no excuse she could give him, no way she could suggest that his mother needed him, not while she was sleeping.

She nodded. 'All right,' she agreed, but her heart was pounding and she didn't know what he was going to say. Probably nothing. She was being silly, it was probably about Linda or work or telling her he was going back to Africa.

He picked up the lead and Digger was there, coiled ready for action, and he clipped it on, opened the door and ushered her out.

'Well?' she asked, unable to bear the suspense any longer. They were up on the headland; they'd walked up Harbour Road to the church at the top of the rise with its pretty lychgate, and now they were heading down to the lighthouse on the end of the promontory, above the cliff. And she couldn't bear it any more.

'Can we sit down?' he suggested, and she looked at the grass. It had been sunny all day, it might be dry enough. And they'd often sat on the headland and talked.

'Sure,' she said, and watched as he lowered himself carefully to the ground and stretched his left leg out in front of him, bending the other one up and wrapping his arms around his knee.

'Sam?' she prompted when he still showed no signs of speaking, but even then he didn't say anything or look at her, just stared out over the sea while Digger sniffed around his feet and finally lay down. And, like the dog, she resigned herself to waiting patiently until he was ready.

'I was wondering,' he began at last. 'We can't turn the clock back, it just doesn't work. We can't pick up where we left off, not really, and as you said, we were just kids then. We're adults now, different people. Different things have happened to us, to shape us, strengthen us—change us. And you're right, we don't know each other. So why don't we start again? Right from the very beginning, back before we ever met, as if we don't know each other, have no history, nothing to beat each other to death with. Just two people, with common career interests, getting to know each other.'

She stared at him, because of all the things she'd expected him to come out with, that wasn't one of them. And odd though it sounded, maybe it could work.

She felt a glimmer of excitement, a flicker of hope. She moistened her lips, took a deep breath and started.

'OK. So—I'm Gemma. I'm a nurse, as you know, and I work in the surgery here, as you know, and I'm twenty-nine, and I'm sort of single—well—am I?' she asked, and he turned his head and smiled a little wryly.

'Yes,' he murmured, his voice low and slightly gruff. 'Yes, you are.'

'OK,' she said, suddenly feeling a little less confident because she hadn't ever thought of herself as single in all this time, more as—a wife on ice? 'So, I'm single, and I like children and animals, and daytime TV when I get a chance, and I read crime fiction and biographies, and I like swimming in the sea but I can't surf to save my life, and I love walking on the moors. How about you?'

He gave her a funny little smile that made her heart turn over again, and said, 'I'm Sam, I'm thirty, I'm a doctor, and I'm covering for an old childhood friend until her replacement can be found, and I've been working in Africa for an aid agency but I did something stupid and got myself blown up, which is why I walk with a limp and can't feel much in my left hand and why—why I've got some pretty horrible scars.

'And my mother's not very well, but because you did your job and checked on her even though you were off duty she's going to be fine, and I'm really grateful, and I'd like to get to know you better. And I'm single, I suppose, but there was a girl a long time ago who broke my heart, so I'm a little wary.'

That made her eyes fill and her heart twist with anguish, and she bit her lip as he went on, 'I love swimming in the sea, and I used to be able to surf but I'd probably fall over now because of my leg, and I read thrillers and crime fiction and car magazines, and I used to ride a motorbike but I can't any longer, but I still love walking on the moors, even though my ankle's not too keen on it. And I have two younger sisters, both married with children, both living fairly near but not apparently near enough to be of much help to my mother, and I have a younger brother who's off the rails a bit but basically a good kid.'

He smiled again. 'And that's me, really. Any questions?'

She shook her head. 'Not really.' Not that she could ask, anyway. Not under the terms and conditions of this new relationship. 'How about you?'

'Are you an only child?'

'No, I've got an older brother, he's thirty-three and he's married with two children, and he lives in Bristol. He's an architect.'

'Interesting. So—did you always want to be a nurse?'

She gave a strangled little laugh, then shook her head. 'No. I was going to be a doctor, like you, but then…' She faltered. Should she tell him? Explain what had happened, why she'd gone? But, no, they were playing let's pretend, and she wouldn't have told a stranger about it, so she carried on, choosing her words carefully, 'Then something happened, and I met some nurses, and I realised I'd rather do that. I'd met lots of doctors, because my father's a doctor so I've grown up round them, but I'd never really had anything to do with nurses before, and the more I talked to them, the more I thought it was a better direction for me.'

Sam was silent, assimilating her words. There was something missing, some gap in her story—something vital. But he didn't know… 'What was it that happened? Was it while you were travelling?'

Oh, rats. Tell him? Or not tell him? She wanted to, but at the same time she didn't, because she was so afraid he'd feel obliged to stand by her, just as she had all those years ago, and she didn't want that. She wanted him for himself, and she wanted him to want her for herself, not feel saddled with her out of duty or a misplaced sense of responsibility.

So she lied—well, no, because it wasn't really a lie, but she was flexible with the truth, and it hurt. 'No, I wasn't travelling at the time, but my circumstances changed and I ended up living amongst nurses.' Well, it was true, in a way. She had, and she'd been there for ages. 'And it changed my conception of them and what they do.'

No. She was still holding something back, still not telling him all of it. But he let it go—for now. He'd get it out of her later, make her tell him everything. For now, he'd let her tell him what she wanted, and he'd try and fill in the blanks.

'So—why practice nurse rather than hospital nurse?'

'For the continuity, really,' she said, relieved to be off the sticky subject of the past and onto something she could talk about with genuine enthusiasm. 'I love the fact that I can watch an entire family grow, from inoculating the babies and giving them advice all through childhood to routine health checks on their parents, and continuing care clinics for the grandparents—like your mother, for example, who comes in regularly for her blood pressure and cholesterol, and Ron Reynolds with his angina, and then there are the children with asthma and the mums who want to give up smoking because they've just found out they're pregnant, and the drop-in contraceptive clinics to keep the youngsters out of trouble and the weight-loss clinics, and the diabetic clinics, and the travel clinics—it's just so varied. Everyone thinks it's just inoculations and smear tests and dressings, but it's not. It's fascinating, and it's all about the people. And it's the people who make the job.'

She looked at him again. 'Does that answer your question?' she asked, and he gave a slight smile.

'Yes, I think it probably does.' For now…

'Can I ask you something now?'

'Sure.'

'Why Africa?'

He looked away, his smile vanishing. 'Why not? God knows, there's a need.'

'But not everybody goes. Why you?'

'Because I was—single? Because nobody was going to be hurt if I was?'

'Except your mother. She was terribly upset.' And me…

He shrugged. 'Accidents can happen to anyone.'

'But that wasn't an accident, Sam. It was a booby trap laid by insurgents.'

'Whatever. I gave the people much more back than was taken from me during the time I was there, and that's what matters. I remember one occasion when I had to contact a colleague in London and ask for advice on a procedure I'd never done before, and the only way to contact him was by mobile phone. We had satellite phones, and he was able to text me instructions. And I saved this kid's life because of that. Without me, without the team, without people going out there and having a go in often impossible conditions, these children and their mothers and fathers would die. And it's the simple things—like appendicitis and not having clean water and not having basic antibiotics and anti-malarials that kills them so often. And I was able to make a difference.'

'And you don't think you can make a difference here? What about Ron Reynolds? If you hadn't been there in the surgery when he'd come in, he might have died.'

'No, because Hazel would have got you, and you would have taken one look at him and called an ambulance, and got Nick back from fiddling with the barbeque arrangements and he would have been fine. But there are kids out in Africa now who are dying because I'm not there.'

'Sam, that's nonsense, because if you're there, then there are children dying in India or Indonesia or South America or Birmingham or even Cornwall because you aren't there. You can't save the world. You can only do your bit.'

He turned and searched her face, then his eyes softened in a smile that made her breath catch. 'You know, you're beautiful when you get worked up about something. You come alive inside, and your skin glows and your eyes are bright and—you're just gorgeous.'

She felt her skin warm, and she couldn't stop the slightly embarrassed little laugh that escaped from her chest. 'Sam…'

'I want to kiss you,' he said softly. 'Will you let me?'

She nodded, speechless with need and emotion, and, leaning over, he angled his head and touched his lips to hers.

Just gently, just the lightest touch, but it struck a spark to the tinder of her withered, lonely heart and brought it to life. But all too soon he was lifting his head and moving away, his eyes still locked with hers.

'Can I see you again?'

She nodded. 'Of course.'

'Tonight?' He closed his eyes. 'Damn, no, I can't tonight, I promised I'd go up to the Carters' for a drink later. You could come?'

She shook her head. 'No. I don't think so. I think this should just be between us.'

A shadow crossed his face. 'Yes, of course. I was forgetting. Saturday, then? Saturday night. We could—I don't know, we could go out of town somewhere.'

'Or I could cook for you,' she suggested, and then wondered if that was too much, too soon. 'Or we could just go for a walk.'

'We could go for a walk and then you could cook for me another time.'

She smiled. 'That's two dates.'

'Mmm.' He smiled back. 'It is. Well?'

She nodded, still smiling. 'Yes. Let's go for a walk on Saturday, if it's not raining.'

'And if it is?'

She shrugged. 'We could go to the cinema?'

'And sit in the back row?'

The little bubble of laughter wouldn't stay down. They'd done that so often when they'd first started going out together. And he'd taken full advantage of the darkness…

'Maybe. If you promise to be good.'

'Oh, I'll be good,' he vowed, and she felt her heart stutter in her chest.

She sucked in a deep breath. 'OK. We'll do that, then. Walk or cinema, and then on Sunday I'll cook for you.'

He pulled a face. 'I should probably be at home on Sunday, cooking a roast for my mother. Sunday is always a roast, or it always used to be. And if I cook it, there's a fair chance it won't be drowned in saturated fat and there'll be lots of fresh vegetables.'

She cocked her head on one side. 'That sounds very civilised.'

'Oh, I can be—when the occasion demands it, I can be very civilised. But most of the time it's something fast, cheap and easy.'

She laughed. 'That sounds a little suspect,' she teased, and he chuckled.

'Well, if the cap fits…' He turned back to the dog and scratched his ears. 'Shall we go back to Mum, little man?'

Digger jumped up, tail wagging, and Sam got stiffly to his feet, flexing his left leg which was obviously giving him trouble still.

'Are you sure you're OK for a walk on Saturday?' she asked, and he shot her a curious look.

'Yes—why?'

'I just wondered. Your leg?'

'My leg's OK. I have to keep using it. It's getting better all the time, and a walk will be just what it needs. And Digger will have a great time, won't you, mate?'

They walked back to the house side by side, not quite touching but close enough for little electric currents to zing between them, and when he slipped his hand behind her back to usher her across the road she felt the warmth of it curl through her, right down to her toes.

'Have you got everything?' he asked as she stopped by her car, and she nodded.

'Yes, I picked it all up on the way out.'

'I'll just put the dog in and move my car, then.'

She unlocked her car and got in, wondering if he'd kiss her again, but instead he opened his car door once the dog was safely inside, fired up the engine and moved out into the road so she could get out, and then he gave her a lazy, sexy wink and a wave as she moved off up the hill.

It was going to be a long time till Saturday...

CHAPTER SIX

FRIDAY was busy, and Gemma hardly saw Sam.

Probably just as well, she told herself, as she wasn't sure she could control her reaction to him well enough in front of patients, but it was curious to know that he was in the room just below her. Curious and comforting, in an oddly exciting way. But then she saw him go out on his visits just before lunch, and wondered how the surgery could suddenly feel so empty.

Ridiculous.

But in her heart was a little bubble of hope, and she kept seeing that little sexy wink and the waggle of his fingers as he'd waved her off last night, and she couldn't wait till tomorrow.

'Right, that should be OK for a few days, but if you have any trouble, come back to me on Monday,' she said to Mrs Jacobs as she smoothed the dressing firmly into place over her leg ulcer. It was healing well, and hopefully the dressings could come off altogether soon.

She glanced at her watch as she showed Mrs Jacobs out of the door. Ten to twelve. Time for a bit of paperwork—mostly reminders for smear tests and well-person checks, baby inoculations and so on. Necessary, but dull, and not the part of her job she liked best, by any means.

Still, she had a good clinic this afternoon, a nice mix of young and old, well and not so well. And with any luck, it would make the day whiz by and take her mind off Sam for long enough that she could do her job!

'Sam?'

He stopped on the path of his patient's bungalow and looked in at the intimidatingly familiar face of his old headmistress in the window next door.

She was tapping on the glass, and she beckoned him in with an imperious finger. He felt a smile curve his lips, and without ceremony he crossed the grass, tapped on the door and went in. 'Well, hello, you,' he said, crossing over to her and crouching down beside her chair. 'How are you? You look well.'

'I'm very well. Back in my home at last—have you got time for a cup of tea?'

He glanced at his watch. He did, but only if he didn't stop for lunch at the practice—which meant not seeing Gemma. But he could live with that. It would heighten the suspense—as if that was necessary! But Gertrude Stanbury had been one of the very few people who'd believed in him, Nick being the other most significant one, and he owed old Gertie a damn sight more than the time for a cup of tea. Not that he'd get that if she heard him refer to her as Gertie!

'That would be lovely,' he said with genuine warmth, and he stood back and watched as she struggled to her feet and limped painfully into the kitchen.

'You're in pain,' he said, and she turned and raised that autocratic brow at him as of old.

'And just who are you to tell me that?'

He grinned. 'Ah, well, it was a medical comment.'

'Was it, indeed? I've had a knee replacement, and I need the other one done. Going to fast-track me?'

He chuckled. 'You know I would if I could, but it wouldn't be fair and, anyway, I'm only locuming. I have as much clout as you do, probably a damn sight less. So—how are you really?'

'Oh, not so good, but I manage. Sam, could you put the kettle on for me? I find it hard to lift if there's more than just a cupful in.'

'Sure.'

He wondered how on earth she did manage, and asked.

'Oh, I have a home help who's marvellous, and I get by. But I'm all the better for seeing you back home. I'm sorry about your mother. I gather she's made excellent progress.'

'She has. Who's your spy?'

She chuckled. 'Lauren. She came to put me through my paces this morning. Sam, could you pass me down those cups, please?'

'Sure. I gather you had to move out after the flood.'

'I did, but it's done me a huge favour. I've got new furniture and carpets and everywhere's redecorated—it's like a new house, and yet all my precious things were safe, because they were in the top of a wardrobe. And the rest…' She shrugged and smiled. 'Well, I won't have to worry about replacing anything again in my lifetime. The insurance company were wonderful. So—tell me about Africa. What's this I hear about you having an accident?'

'Nothing passes you by, does it?' he said gently,

taking the carefully laid tray from the worktop and following her into her sitting room.

'Not much, but I can see that you survived it, more or less. I gather young Jamie's in trouble, though, talking of things that don't pass me by,' she went on. 'You want to keep him away from Gary Lovelace. I don't often give up on a child, as you know, but—well, some people are just plain bad, and I'm afraid he might be one of them. Keep him away from him, Sam, before something awful happens.'

He sighed. 'I don't know if I can. I can threaten, cajole, bribe—but it has to come from him. And I can't find the motivator.'

'I think it all stems from your father leaving—just as yours did. That sense of abandonment—and then you left, when he was six, and now his mother's ill and could so easily have died—he's just scared to love, Sam, scared to care.'

Hell, he knew that feeling so well. He was aching to be back with Gemma, but he was so afraid to trust her, and there was something she wasn't telling him.

'How's it going with Gemma?'

He narrowed his eyes. What the hell did Gertie Stanbury know about Gemma? Could she read his mind? Apparently, because she went on, 'Oh, come on, Sam! I know you loved her—and I know she loved you. And ever since she came back to Penhally, I've been waiting for you to come home. I knew you would. You all do, in the end.'

'Maybe,' he said, and then changed the subject—or at least, the subject of the subject. 'What do you remember about Polly Searle?'

'Oh, dear, that poor child. Little mouse. She had the

most dreadful home life—awful man, her father. I was so worried what would become of her after her mother died. I thought she'd waste away at one point but she always had brains, just like you. Thank goodness she got away and she's all right. She'll be a marvellous doctor—a really good listener. Not enough people are, you know. Kate Althorp was wonderful to her, and I think they're still in touch. She's her godmother, I believe. Why do you ask?'

'Kate was talking about her. We need a woman doctor and Kate was suggesting she might be available.'

'Oh. Well, I don't know if she'll come back. It'll take a lot of courage, but she was never short of that.'

Sam tried to remember, but his image of Polly was blurred by time and had never been a strong one. 'Oh, well, time will tell, I suppose,' he said, and got to his feet. 'I need to get on. It's lovely to see you again.'

'You haven't told me about your accident.'

He grinned. 'No, that's right, I haven't. I'll have to come back again.'

'You do that, young man. You're always welcome in my house. And good luck with Gemma.'

He opened his mouth to correct her, but then shut it again and smiled. 'Thank you. And you take care of yourself. I'll see you soon.'

'Bring me good news!' she called as she watched him down the path, and he laughed and waved her goodbye, then got back into his car and drove down to the surgery, listening to the weather forecast as he went.

Tomorrow was going to be warm and sunny, with light winds and the odd bit of high cloud. Pity, he thought with a wry smile. He'd been looking forward to the cinema…

* * *

'Kate? It's Rob.'

'Oh, hi, Rob.' Kate cradled the phone against her ear and watched Jem through the open door to the sitting room. 'What can I do for you?'

'I was just wondering what you and Jem are doing today. I was hoping to see you to ask you last night at school, but you weren't there.'

'No, I'm sorry, I was working late—but we haven't any plans today,' she told him, wondering what he was going to suggest and discovering that she was actually looking forward to it, whatever it might turn out to be. 'What did you have in mind?'

'A bike ride. It's so lovely, I thought I'd take Matthew up onto Bodmin, and I wondered if you'd like to join us?'

'Oh. That would be really nice—although I can't remember when I last rode my bike. Jem's is getting a bit small for him. I'm going to have to get another one soon, I think, because he's growing like a weed. Maybe for his birthday—actually, that's a good idea. It's this month. Perhaps you can give me some guidance, because I really don't know what's good for kids or not.'

Rob chuckled. 'No problem. So I'll pick up the school minibus with the bike rack on the back and come and get you—what time?'

'How about ten? Does that give you long enough? Either then or later, so it's not too hot—and I could bring a picnic.'

'That would be really nice. I'll see you at ten, then.'

She hung up, a little smile playing around her mouth, and went through to the sitting room. Jem looked up as she walked in. 'Who was that, Mum?'

'Mr Werrick. He wondered if we'd like to go for a bike ride up on Bodmin.'

'Cool! Can we go?'

'I said yes—and we're going to take a picnic, so you need to check the tyres on both our bikes while I have a look and see what I can find in the fridge.'

'Tuna sandwiches,' Jem yelled, running out of the back door, 'and chocolate biscuits!'

'OK!' And humming, Kate took out the bread and set to work.

It was glorious up on Bodmin.

Glorious because, with the wind in her hair and Sam at her side, she could have been eighteen again, back in the days when nothing had troubled them and everything had seemed wonderful.

They'd ridden out across the moors on his big, powerful bike the summer he'd met her, when she'd only been seventeen and he eighteen, dark and dangerously exciting in his black leathers with the shadow of stubble on his jaw and that wickedly enticing twinkle in his eyes, and they'd lain in the heather and kissed for hours on end, till her lips were full and swollen and her skin was raw from stubble rash, but she wouldn't go any further. Not until she was married. She was saving herself—it was a promise she'd made to herself ages ago, and she'd meant it, but hadn't stopped Sam trying everything else that he could think of, and he'd had an amazing imagination.

But it hadn't been enough, and so the second summer, after a frustrating year of letters and phone calls during term time and seeing her only when she was down in Penhally with her parents at their holiday cottage, he'd asked her to marry him, in a crazy moment, and she'd been so stunned and so in love with him she'd said yes.

They'd been up here on the moor when he'd asked her. Lying on a picnic rug, hearts racing, their bodies screaming for that last step that she wouldn't take, and she'd often wondered if he would have asked her if she hadn't held out, or if their affair would just have fizzled out.

But he had asked her, and it seemed incredible now that they'd gone through with it. She'd gone home to Bath on the pretext of needing some more clothes and had tracked down her birth certificate, and they'd gone straight to the registrar and arranged it, booked a time for the first legal opportunity just sixteen days later, and then, without telling anyone, they'd made their vows, with Jack and Lucy Tremayne, sworn to secrecy, as their witnesses.

They'd spent forty-eight hours of hedonistic bliss in the ramshackle beach house he was renting just a mile along from the centre of the village, and with incredible patience and restraint, Sam had gently, tenderly, shown her just what her body was capable of. They'd had so much fun, shed tears of laughter and of joy, eating, sleeping, talking and above all making love again and again and again, and then reality had intruded with a thunderous knock at the door in the middle of the night, and her parents had stood there, incandescent with rage. And telling them they were married didn't help. At all.

'Hey, what's up?'

She dragged herself out of the past and looked up at him, still miles away. 'Nothing,' she said, blinking away the bitter-sweet memories of that long-ago summer. 'Just remembering.'

'Remembering?' he said, a teasing light in his eyes. 'Have you been here before, then?'

And she reminded herself that they were starting

again, without the past, without the hang-ups and heart-aches, and she smiled a little mischievously. 'Oh, once or twice, but I was much younger then. I always loved it up here. How about you?'

'Likewise—but I have to say the present's every bit as good,' he murmured.

She gazed up into his eyes, her breath lodged in her throat, and then he seemed to free himself from his trance and reached back into the car. 'Here, I brought us some lunch. We can take it with us and find some-where to sit and eat it.'

'Oh! How lovely! Thanks, Sam. Let me take it, you've got the dog.' And he couldn't manage both, not with his torn shoulder.

'Thanks. Wretched dog. He needs to learn not to go down holes so I can let him off for a run. It took five days to dig him out last time, and he was lucky to survive, apparently. Personally, I would have left him there, wouldn't I, Digger?'

Digger wriggled his tail and grinned, tongue lolling, lead taut as he stood poised for his walk, and Sam grinned back and locked the car and headed off along the path with Gemma at his side.

They walked over the rise, not too far because of his ankle, listening to the sound of the curlews and the bleating of the sheep, and then they settled down with their faces to the sun and their backs to an outcrop of granite, and ate their lunch.

'This is gorgeous,' she said round a mouthful of smoked-salmon sandwich, and he grinned.

'Ah, well, a little bird told me you like smoked salmon,' he teased. Stealing her sandwich from her hand, he opened it, peeled out the salmon and dangled it over her mouth. 'Open wide,' he instructed, and then slowly lowered it to her lips.

She took it from him, their eyes locked, and he threw the bread to the dog who was poised waiting.

'Mmm,' she said, licking her lips, and his eyes darkened, his breath hissing out and touching her face. Another inch, she thought. Just another inch, and his lips…

The contact brought a shuddering sigh from his chest, and she could feel his hand trembling against her cheek.

'God, Gemz, I want you,' he breathed, and she heard a whimper of longing—hers? Oh, yes, hers, a longing for the touch of his body, for the feel of his skin against hers, for the weight of him poised over her, his solid, muscled body trembling with restraint.

His hand slid up under her T-shirt and cupped her breast, and she arched up into his palm, aching for him just as she had all those years ago. But it was worse now, harder to hold back, because she knew what she was missing, knew just what his touch had to offer, what his body could do to hers and the heights it could take her to, but she couldn't let him, couldn't go there again, not without telling him…

Sam hauled himself back under control. He couldn't do this. Not up here, on the moor, where anybody could walk past and see them. They weren't kids any longer, they were adults—married to each other, for heaven's sake, although now that was little more than a technicality, he thought with regret—but he needed her. God, how he needed her, the healing touch of her hands on his body, the tender kisses, the sweet sighs, the fractured little screams as she neared her peak, and it was driving him mad.

'Gemz? Let's get out of here,' he groaned softly. 'I want to make love to you, and I'm not doing it with an audience of sheep and ponies and dog-walkers.'

'We can't, Sam.'

'Why not? Give me one good reason why not.'

She swallowed and forced herself to meet his eyes with an unsteady smile. 'Because we've only just met.'

She saw confusion in his eyes, then frustration and then, finally, irony. He laughed softly and dropped onto his back beside her, his wry chuckle making her smile. 'Oh, you witch. Really?'

Her smile faded. 'Really, Sam,' she said quietly. 'There's still a lot we don't know about each other. So many things have happened, so much water under the bridge—'

She broke off and he searched her face for clues. *So many things have happened.*

But what things? And why—?

'Digger, no! Come back! Oh, hell.'

He leapt up, letting out a sharp groan and clutching his thigh, and headed off after the dog. 'Digger, damn it, come back here!'

But Digger had seen something, and he was off. Gemma scrambled to her feet and ran after them both, and then watched in horror as the terrier leapt into the path of a group of cyclists and tried to bite the front wheel of the leading bike.

The bike wobbled, all the others swerved and crashed, and the first bike arced through the air and landed on top of the child in the heather.

Oh, lord, she thought, and, racing past Sam, she arrived to a scene of chaos and sobbing, with Kate Althorp in the middle of it.

'Kate! I'm so sorry, he's a naughty dog. Digger, come here, baby. Good boy.' She caught the limping dog and held him while Sam went to the child who'd fallen off. Jem, she thought. It's Jem. She didn't recognise the other boy, or the man who was hovering over him, but she knew Kate's son, and she heaved a sigh of relief as he got to his feet, flexing his wrist and trying not to cry.

'Are you all right, Jem?' Kate was asking, and he nodded.

'How's Matthew?'

'He's fine,' the man said. 'He's banged his shin but I think he's all right.'

'Here, Jem, let me have a look. I'm a doctor,' Sam was saying gently, feeling the boy's forearm and wrist carefully with his fingers. 'I think it's OK, but it's hard to tell. It could be a sprain. If you can come down to the surgery, I'll X-ray it for you and check, and we can plaster it if necessary, but I don't think it will be. I'm just so sorry—I was distracted, and the dog just got away from me.'

Distracted by kissing Gemma, who was standing a few feet away from him looking shaken. Idiot. He should have tied the dog's lead to his foot, not just assumed that the promise of food would be enough to keep him there.

'It's all right, accidents happen,' Kate said; but Gemma could see she was shaking as she bent over her son. 'All right, my love?'

Jem nodded, sniffing a little and struggling to be brave, and Kate said, 'I'm sorry, I should introduce everyone. This is Rob Werrick and his son Matthew, and this is my son Jeremiah. Rob, this is Sam Cavendish, our locum doctor, and Gemma, our practice nurse.'

'Sam—of course,' Rob said, nodding at him. 'I should have recognised you, you're the spitting image of your brother.'

Sam grunted. Was he? Of course he was—and they were both the spitting image of their father, although he'd left his mother because he didn't believe Jamie was his, of all the ironies. And now was not the time to get into that.

'Where's your car?' he asked, and Rob jerked his head towards the top of the hill.

'Up there—it's next to a silver hire car. Is that yours?'

'Yes. So we're going in the same direction. How are we going to get us all back there?'

'I'll go and get the van—it's the school minibus, it'll go over these tracks. I won't be long. Matt, stay here with Jem and Kate, and I'll be as quick as I can, all right?'

He nodded, and his father set off for the car park at a run, and they settled down to wait. Sam glanced at the injured boy, and felt a vague flicker of recognition. Jem looked familiar, but he couldn't work out why. He was nothing like James Althorp, that was for sure, but he reminded him so clearly of someone…

'Why don't we sit down and wait for him?' he suggested, and they all sank down on the heather, the bikes still lying where they'd fallen, and Gemma brought the dog over to him, a worried look in her eyes.

'Sam, I'm not sure, but I think Digger might be hurt.'

'Oh, no! I didn't mean to hurt him!' Jem said, sounding worried, but Sam just gave him a rueful smile.

'It's hardly your fault, Jem. He's a rascal. Digger, come here, boy, let me see.'

But he was holding his paw up, and Sam could see without getting closer that it was swelling.

'I think it might have got run over,' he said quietly. 'Silly, silly dog. That'll teach you to chase bikes. We'll have to take you to the vet later.'

'You can go now. Uncle Nick can X-ray my arm,' Jem said. 'He won't mind.'

Uncle Nick? Or...?

The recognition was sudden and startling, and Sam let out his breath on a quiet, surprised sigh and turned back to the dog while he assimilated the information. Nick and Kate? Really? When?

'Mum, I think my bike's broken.'

'Oh, no,' Sam groaned. 'Look, I'll pay for a new one, OK?'

'No, you won't,' Kate said with a smile. 'It was too small for him anyway. I was going to buy him a new one for his birthday—it's this month.'

May. Nine months after August. So that summer, the summer he and Gemma had got married, the summer of the storm, Nick and Kate had been having an affair?

God. Had Annabel known? Had Jack, or Lucy, or Ed?

No. Surely not? There'd been no sign—not that he would have noticed, he admitted, because he'd been so wrapped up in Gemma the world could have fallen apart and they wouldn't have noticed.

The sound of an engine interrupted his thoughts, and the minibus appeared over the rise and bumped its way down to them. Minutes later they were packed up and away, and although the dog was injured, Sam insisted that they drive down to the surgery to make sure Jem was all right before they took Digger to the vet.

They were met by Nick, who examined the boy's arm and X-rayed it with a curious detachment that Sam found puzzling. Almost as if he was keeping his distance…

'Well, it's just a sprain, I think,' Nick said, and Sam, looking at the X-ray over his shoulder, nodded in relief and turned back to the others, to see Rob's gaze flicking curiously from Nick to Jem and back again. So he can see it, too, Sam thought. It's not just me. And who else has worked it out? Did Nick know? Surely to God he must?

But it was none of his business, and he forced himself to concentrate. 'Thank heavens for that,' he said, and smiled at the boy apologetically. 'I'm really sorry, Jem, but I'll make sure you get a new bike out of it, OK? It's the least I can do. Right, if it's OK with you all, I need to take the wretched dog to the vet now,' he said. 'Who do I call?'

'Oh, that'll be Melinda Lovac. Dragan was complaining that she was on call and so he'd be left with a grizzly baby,' Gemma said with a smile. 'He's teething, and he's had a cold. Give her a ring—here, we've got her number,' she said, and, going behind Reception, she looked it up, dialled the number and handed him the receiver, then went to put a support bandage on Jeremiah's arm.

'Oh, Digger! What a smart paw!' Gemma said, popping in later to see how he was and admiring his bandage. 'And what a lovely hat!'

'Idiot dog,' Sam grumbled as Digger turned round and smashed the clear plastic Elizabethan collar into his leg. 'How's Jem?'

'Fine. He's a bit sore, but I've put a support on it and he's OK, and everyone else is all right. Matthew's got a little bruise on his shin but, apart from that, the only other damage is to Jem's bike.'

'I still think I should replace it.'

'No. Kate's insistent she's buying him one for his birthday.'

'Well, she can, but I'm paying for it,' he said stubbornly, and Gemma chuckled.

'I'll let you two sort it out between you,' she said, knowing just how stubborn Kate could be, too. 'So what happened to his paw?'

'Fractured metacarpal. Melinda said he'll be fine, but he needs to keep the bandage on as long as possible— which will be as long as we can stand him crashing into things in that lampshade. Hopefully it'll teach him a lesson, but I'm not holding my breath. He's a terrier, and terriers are born to chase and to dig. He does both, with knobs on!' He tipped his head over to one side. 'So— we never got to finish lunch,' he said softly, 'and there's the remains of the picnic sitting in the cool box in my car. How's about going down to the beach to finish it? Without the dog?'

'Oh, Digger, he's so mean to you!' she murmured, scratching his head inside the collar, and then she straightened up with a smile and met his eyes. His sexy, smouldering, midnight-blue eyes. And then she remembered what they were doing, what he was saying, when the dog had run off, and her heart pounded.

'That sounds lovely,' she said, and she pulled herself together with effort. They were supposed to be getting to know each other all over again—but not that fast! And there was so much she needed to tell him before she let him get that close, but they should be safe on the beach. 'But I can't stop for long,' she added. 'I've got lots to do.'

Which was a total lie, because she'd cleaned her house until it squeaked the previous weekend, apart from the ironing—well, OK, the ironing was still there, and would take her the rest of this weekend, so it wasn't really a lie, except that now she'd have to do it!

'Come on, then, we'll take the car. All that running over rough ground hasn't done my ankle any good. I reckon Lauren will kill me.'

'No, she won't. She'll just sigh and fix it,' she said, and followed him out of the door, leaving the disappointed dog behind.

They drove up over the rise past the church and the Smugglers' Inn, and then past the surfing beach and on to the next cove, to the beach where Sam had been camping out in the tumbledown little wooden shack all those summers ago.

The place where they'd spent their honeymoon, she thought, with the single bed against the wall and a Primus stove to cook on and not much else, but it had been home, for one glorious and utterly romantic weekend. It wasn't there any more, of course. It had been in a terrible state even then, and she imagined it had fallen to pieces long ago.

'There used to be a little cabin here on stilts, just on the edge of the beach, by the sand dunes,' she said softly, carrying on their game of let's pretend as they settled down on the sand with their backs to a rock. 'Along there, at the end.'

He met her eyes, his expression sombre. 'Yes. It got smashed to bits in a storm, just after my…' He hesitated, then went on, 'Just after the girl I loved left me.'

She felt tears fill her eyes. She hadn't known that. Hadn't known that the house had been destroyed by the storm, that Sam could have been in it, that everything inside must have been washed into the sea. And all those memories...

'I'm sorry,' she said, her heart aching for him, because it had been his retreat, the place he came to escape the pressures of home. And for those few days, it had been like living in paradise. 'Were you—were you here? When it happened?'

'No. I was up in the village, trying to help get the kids off the rocks,' he said bleakly, remembering how he'd helped them, how he'd watched James Althorp being washed away, and Nick's brother Phil being smashed against the cliff by a huge wave, but none of it had reached him because he'd been numb inside, so over-whelmed with pain because she'd left him that he'd shut down. 'I didn't think about the house at all. But then I went back later, and it was gone, everything washed away, just broken matchwood flung up on the foreshore and a few bits of clothing lying around in the seaweed like so much flotsam. I didn't come here again for years.'

'Oh, Sam. I'm so sorry.'

He smiled, a fleeting, sad smile, and shook his head. 'Don't be. It was a long time ago, and nothing to do with us.'

Really? He was still persisting with that? OK. She took a deep, steadying breath and prodded the cool box with her foot. 'So are you going to feed me, then, or is this going to be yet another occasion when you tease me with food and then leave me hungry?' she said lightly, and he gave a soft huff of laughter and pulled the lid off.

'Oh, I don't want to leave you hungry, Gemma.

That's not my style. Not my style at all. So—what do you fancy?'

You, she thought, her heart thumping. I want you, Sam. Nothing else. Nothing more. Just you. But I don't know if I can have you, and I don't know if it's fair to ask…

CHAPTER SEVEN

SUNDAY was dull.

Gemma spent the whole day ironing and daydreaming about Sam, and the night doing the other sort of dreaming—the sort of dreaming that had been more and more frequent since he'd come back, and which, since Saturday's kiss, had started to spiral out of control.

And on Monday morning she went back to work, and he was the first person she saw, coming upstairs to the staffroom to grab a cup of tea before his surgery.

'You don't have to do that, my duck, I'll bring it down to you in a moment. You go on,' Doris said, fussing around him, and Sam thanked her and shot Gemma a wry smile over her head—a smile that said had they been alone, there might have been another kiss.

She went into her room and was buzzed almost immediately.

'Morning, gorgeous,' he murmured in a wonderfully growly purr that sent a shiver down her spine. 'How's the ironing?'

'Done,' she said with a smile. 'How was the roast?'

'Good—except that Jamie went out straight afterwards and didn't get home till three. I had to drag him out of bed again this morning—but you don't need to hear that. I just wanted to tell you—oh, thank you, Doris, put it there, that's great.' He paused, and she heard his door click shut before he went on in that deep, persuasive rumble, 'My mother's got an appointment at the hospital today, so I'll be going in after lunch with her and then after that I'm free, and you did mention the other day that you'd cook for me at some point, so I thought tonight might be a good opportunity…'

She squashed a smile. 'Are you inviting yourself to dinner, Dr Cavendish?'

She could hear his answering smile down the phone. 'Do you know, Nurse Johnson, I believe I might be?'

And then there was a funny silence, while they both thought about that. Because of course she wasn't Johnson any more, but she wasn't Cavendish either, not really, and she wasn't sure if she ever would be again. It took her a second to get her mind back in order, to remind herself that they were playing a game and she needed to stick to the rules, for now at least, and then she took a deep breath and said, 'Well, then, I suppose it would be churlish not to extend a formal invitation, wouldn't it?'

'It might very well be. Seven-thirty or eight?'

'Or earlier. I have to be at work tomorrow morning at eight, so if you don't want to be kicked out the moment you've scraped up the last morsel, you could make it seven.'

'Seven will do nicely. Can I bring anything?'

'Just yourself. You know the way to Seagull Cottage, don't you?'

'I'm sure I'll find it,' he said with a chuckle in his voice. 'I'll see you later.'

'I'll look forward to it.'

She cradled the phone with a smile, and tried to concentrate on her patients, but then a man hobbled into her room and asked if she could put something on his leg to support it, because it was swelling a bit since he'd trapped it between the boats on Friday. Alarm bells rang instantly.

'Friday?' she said. 'But it's Monday.'

'Well, I've been busy, and I didn't think it was anything to worry about really, but it's giving me a bit of stick now.'

'Well, let me have a look,' she said, and when he rolled up his trouser leg she had to stifle a gasp. It was black. Literally black, from the knee down, and she couldn't imagine how much pain he must be in. 'I really think you need to see a doctor with this,' she said, comparing it to his other, undamaged, leg. It was nearly twice the size, and she was worried for the circulation to his foot.

If it wasn't too late to worry. She hoped not. The foot was cool—colder than the other one, but not too much so, and she buzzed Sam and asked him if he could pop up for a moment when he was free.

'I'll come now, you've caught me between patients,' he said, and she heard his uneven tread on the landing and then a sharp tap as he entered.

'This is Mr Polgrean, he trapped his leg between two boats on Friday,' she explained, and Sam took one look at it and nodded briskly.

'Hello there, Mr Polgrean, I'm Dr Cavendish.'

'I know who you are, and your brother's no better. Don't know what your mother's thinking about the way she's let you both run around, causing havoc and making people's lives a misery. I want another doctor. I don't want you anywhere near my leg.'

Sam folded his arms and nodded from the other side of the room, but Gemma could see the withdrawal in his eyes and knew he must be hurt. 'OK. Fair enough. But I'm the only doctor on the premises at the moment, and I don't know if you have any idea of the seriousness of this injury, but even from here I can tell you that there's a possibility you'll lose the leg if you don't get to hospital immediately. I think you have a thing called compartment syndrome—'

'This is no time for one of your jokes, young man,' Mr Polgrean said. 'I know what you're doing, and it won't work.'

Sam ignored him and carried on. 'When you caught your leg between the boats, you bruised it, but there's a problem with that. Each of the muscles in your leg is enclosed in a sheath, and you've sustained such severe injuries to the muscles that they've all swollen and because of the tight sheath around each one, the pressure on the muscles is going to cause them to die. And then you'll lose your leg. And if you ignore it for too long, you could die. Now, clever money would go to hospital and have an operation to cut a little slit in each of the sheaths to reduce the compression on the muscles and save your leg, but if you like, I'll go back downstairs and we can let nature take its course.'

Mr Polgrean stared at Sam for an age and swallowed hard. 'You're just trying to frighten me. You're blinding me with science and trying to scare the living daylights out of me, but I know you and your practical jokes, Sam Cavendish, and I'm not falling for this one.'

'No. I'm not joking,' he said quietly. 'I'm sorry you

don't like me or my family, but that's nothing to do with this. I did a lot of things when I was young that I regret, but I'm not going to let that lead me into doing something else as an adult that I'll regret even more, and if I walk away from you now and you lose your leg, I won't be able to live with myself. And I have to say, dumping several stone of spoilt herring on our drive was pretty good revenge,' he added softly. 'I was clearing it up for days.'

Mr Polgrean grunted, but his leg was obviously extremely painful, and Gemma was getting worried. Sam was standing there waiting, Mr Polgrean was lying with arms folded over his bulky chest and the faint aroma of rotting fish drifting from him, and she wondered what it would take to break the deadlock.

But then he started to chuckle. 'Days?' he said. 'Did it take you that long, boy?'

Sam's mouth twitched. 'It did, and I never forgot it. I thought I'd never get the smell off my hands.'

'I've still got that mermaid painted on my boat,' Mr Polgrean said slowly. 'You did a good job. Best endowed mermaid I ever did see,' he mused, a smile flickering on his face. 'But your brother—'

'My brother is nothing to do with this, and I'm dealing with him.'

'Not fast enough. He was outside last night with that Gary Lovelace, causing all sorts of mayhem. Wonder they weren't all arrested.'

Gemma saw Sam close his eyes and sigh quietly.

'So—what's it to be? Hospital, or sit there and argue until your leg drops off?' It was said quietly, very matter-of-factly, and after a moment the man nodded.

'All right, then. Do your worst, young Dr Cavendish, but I tell you, if I die, I'm coming back to haunt you.'

Sam grinned wryly. 'I don't doubt it, Mr Polgrean. I don't doubt it for a moment.'

The tap on her door was a minute early, but it wouldn't have mattered if he'd been ten minutes early, or ten minutes late, come to that, because she was still in her bedroom vacillating between the blue jeans with a long-sleeved T-shirt, the black trousers with a lacy vest top and a shrug over the top, and a little sundress that was probably too thin for the cool May evening but was so pretty she really, really wanted to wear it.

And now here he was, and she still hadn't made a decision.

'Eeny, meeny, miny, mo,' she said, and grabbed the little dress at random, hauling it over her head and fluffing her hair into place before running downstairs in bare feet.

'Hi,' she said, opening the door, and he came in, took one look at her and dumped the flowers he was carrying and kissed her.

'Hi, yourself,' he murmured when he came up for air. 'You look gorgeous. I brought you some flowers and some of Mum's chocolate stash, in the interests of preventative medicine.'

She chuckled and went up on tiptoe and kissed his cheek. 'Thank you. That's very public spirited of you, and I'll do my best to justify your faith in my ability to protect the community from harm.'

He laughed and pulled her back up against him and kissed her once more, then he freed her slowly and sniffed. 'Something smells good. What are we having?'

'Moules marinière, and fresh home-made bread—well, it will be, when it comes out of the breadmaker—and steak from the Trevellyans' with a green salad and some new potatoes, and I've got a nice bottle of Chablis in the fridge and some Merlot if you'd rather. Except of course you're driving.'

He grinned. 'That's fine. I can still get you tipsy and have my evil way with you,' he murmured, and she felt a quiver of need race through her.

'Ever the gentleman,' she murmured, and turned away to the stove, only to find his arms sneaking round her and easing her up against his hard, muscular body.

'You wouldn't really want that,' he murmured into the angle of her neck, his lips nibbling at her skin.

'Maybe not, but I want to eat first,' she said, and then there was a breathless silence before he reached out and switched off the hob, then turned her slowly into his arms.

'First?' he said, his face taut, his body rigid with tension.

She gave in. 'Oh, Sam,' she whispered, and going up on tiptoe, she cradled his face in her hands and drew him down for her kiss. 'I've missed you so much.'

'Hell, Gemz,' he muttered, and then his mouth was plundering hers, searching it hungrily, his lips moving over her face, her throat, over her collar bones while his right hand slid up inside her dress, dragging it up so he could curl his fingers over her hipbone and haul her closer.

'I need you, Gemma. It's been so damn long and I just want to hold you.'

She eased away from him, took his shaking hand in hers and led him up the steep, narrow staircase to her bedroom. The bed was made, the linen freshly washed and ironed, courtesy of yesterday, and she threw the jeans and trousers off it and then gasped as he seized the hem of her dress and peeled it over her head.

'Oh, God, you look the same,' he said, his eyes, as black as midnight, trailing over her and leaving fire in their wake. 'So lovely—so damned lovely.'

'And you're overdressed,' she said, and heard her voice shake a little.

She reached for his belt and unbuckled it, her hands trembling so much she could hardly shift the zip, and he took over, heeling off his shoes and shucking his jeans and boxers and socks in one smooth movement.

His shirt was next, dragged over his head with a muffled groan as he raised his left arm too high for his torn shoulder to tolerate, but it slowed him down, gave him time to draw breath and get himself back under control before he reached for her again.

Because he wanted to do this right. He had no idea what had been wrong before, but something had, he was sure of it, and he wasn't making any mistakes this time; not if it killed him, but after eleven years his control was hanging by a very frayed and tattered thread.

He held out his arms to her, and she walked straight into them, wrapping her arms around him so that he felt her warm, soft body against his for the first time in so long, and he gave a shuddering sigh.

'God, I've missed you. That feels so good,' he mumbled into her hair. 'So soft, so warm. Gemma—'

'Shh. Come on,' she said. Taking him by the hand again, she led him to the bed and turned back the covers, then lay down beside him and drew him into her arms and lifted her face to his.

Oh, dear heaven, it felt so good to hold him, to kiss him, to hold his big, strong body against hers after so long.

She was shaking all over, and she could feel the tremors running through him every time she touched him.

And she did touch him. She had to, her hands greedy for the feel of him, starved of his touch for too long. Their mouths sought each other, their breath mingling on gasps and sighs as they each rediscovered yet another place, another area of skin that seemed suddenly unreasonably sensitive.

And then he was moving over her, his body shaking as he held himself poised above her, his eyes burning like black coals as they held hers and he entered her with one long, slow, steady thrust that took her clean over the edge.

'Sam!' she screamed, and he drove into her, again and again and again, until with a savage, agonised cry he followed her into oblivion.

'I'm starving. All I can smell is that fresh bread, and I am so damn hungry my stomach's attacking me.'

She chuckled and lifted herself up on one elbow, staring down into his eyes. They were smoky now, the pupils back to normal, the expression slaked—for now, at least, as other needs took over.

'I'd better go down to the kitchen and get stuck in, then, hadn't I?' she said. Throwing off the covers, she pulled her sundress on over her head and padded down the stairs, turning on the stove again and throwing the mussels into the pan on top of the softened onions and garlic and humming softly.

She was stirring them when he appeared, dressed only in his jeans, with the top button undone and that delicious arrow of hair tempting her to follow it down...

'Don't look at me like that or we won't eat tonight and I swear I really will fade away.'

'Yeah, right,' she said, but she turned back to the stove, smiling to herself, and he came up behind her and inspected the food over her shoulder.

'If you want a job, you could take the bread out of the breadmaker, but mind you don't burn yourself.'

'I'm not six,' he reprimanded gently, tipping the golden, steaming loaf out onto the breadboard. 'Wow. I could just rip it in half and eat it.'

'And die. Back off. You can open the wine, I need some for the sauce.'

'Nag, nag, nag,' he grumbled, but he did as she'd asked and handed her the bottle.

'Here, pick out the ones that haven't opened and chuck them,' she said, tipping out the mussels and throwing the wine and cream into the pan.

He leant over her shoulder and sniffed. 'Oh, that smells so good. Funny, I've never thought of you as domesticated, but it works, you know? I think I could go for that, the whole barefoot and pregnant in the kitchen thing—'

He broke off, then swore softly. 'Oh, hell, Gemz. I didn't think about that before.'

She felt a shiver of something that could have been fear but could just as easily have been hope, and her eyes filled. If only it was so simple. If only she could just assume, like everybody else...

'Don't worry, it's a safe time,' she said, without going into details, and kept her eyes firmly fixed on the bubbling sauce.

He grunted, then handed her back the sorted mussels and held out the bowls as she dished up. 'Shall I cut the bread?'

'Mmm—big hunks, but not too big because we've still got the steak to come, and then there's the chocolate.'

'We'll see. We may have to have an inter-course break.'

She spluttered with laughter. 'Did you mean that quite like that?' she asked, and he grinned wickedly.

'I believe I meant it exactly like that. Eat up, I want to take you back to bed, my lovely girl. We've got a lot of catching up to do.'

It was nearly ten before they ate the steak, meltingly tender and bursting with flavour, and Sam thought he'd never tasted anything so good in his life. He pushed the plate away and met her eyes.

'That was fan-tastic,' he said slowly, and smiled. 'Utterly gorgeous. Beautiful. Sexy as hell.'

'Are we still talking about the steak here?' she asked, and he chuckled.

'Probably not. But that was pretty special, too.' He glanced at his watch. 'I wonder if Jamie's home?'

'Was he meant to be?'

'After last night? Damn right. I gave him hell, courtesy of Mr Polgrean.'

'What was all that about a mermaid, by the way?' she asked, fascinated. 'What *did* you do to his boat?'

'Ah,' he said, and grinned. 'Yeah, well, there were some marks on the paintwork, and they just suggested this shape to me, so I got some paint—proper marine paint, not any old stuff—and I painted a mermaid over the marks. And she—ah—she was a bit generous in the—ah…'

'Top-heavy?'

He frowned thoughtfully. 'Not really. Just very, very lush.'

'Not like me, then,' she said, wondering if it was utterly unreasonable to be jealous of a mermaid, but Sam just laughed.

'Nothing like you. For a start, you don't have scaly legs.'

'Thank God for that!'

He laughed again, and then getting up he cleared the table, put the plates into the dishwasher and pulled her to her feet. 'I think it's time for chocolate.'

'In the sitting room?'

'No—upstairs,' he said, smiling. 'Go up and wait for me.'

So she went up and sat in the middle of the bed, still in her sundress, and he came up a few minutes later with a tray.

'What on earth have you got there?'

'Grapes, apple, banana and chocolate. Melted chocolate.'

'Oh, wow. DIY chocolate fondue.'

'Exactly. And I'll feed you, but first you have to take off your dress.'

'Done,' she said, flinging it aside. 'I'll have apple first.'

'Uh-uh. We haven't started yet. Lie down.'

She lay, and he picked up a slice of apple, dipped it in the chocolate and dangled it over her mouth. 'Open—now suck.'

She sucked, and his eyes widened.

'Oh, hell, this is not going to work.'

'Works for me,' she mumbled round the apple.

He sighed and dipped a slice of banana into the bowl and trailed the warm chocolate over her chest, then licked it away, and she shivered. He did it again, but then his tongue encountered a little bump in the skin, and he licked it clean and looked at it. A tiny scar. He didn't remember it, but there was plenty of time in eleven years for her to have picked up a scar. He pressed his lips to it and lifted his head, meeting her eyes with a smile.

'Get the idea?'

'Oh, yes,' she said, and, taking her finger and dipping it into the chocolate, she tipped him onto his back and dribbled it down his chest and across the flat, taut plane of his abdomen before putting her finger into her mouth so she could suck it clean while he watched her through narrowed eyes, his breath hissing through his teeth. Then slowly, inch by inch, she followed the dark, glossy trail down his ribs, scooping it up with her tongue while he lay and groaned.

'This was a lousy idea,' he muttered.

She lifted her head and grinned at him mischievously. 'You think? I've never had so much fun with chocolate.'

She straddled him and reached for another fingerful of warm temptation, and as she stroked it over his dark, flat nipples they pebbled under her fingertip and she felt his body harden even more.

'I want you.'

'I know. I can feel.'

'I love you, Gemz,' he said then, and she stopped, her finger halfway to the sauce, and tears filled her eyes.

'Oh, Sam, I love you, too. I've never stopped loving you.'

'Then why—? Oh, hell, what now?'

She stared at him, and then gradually the sound of his mobile phone got through to her. She moved off him, and he sat up and reached for his jeans, pulling the phone out of his pocket with a short sigh.

'Jamie. What the hell does he want?' He flipped the phone open. 'Yeah, hi. What is it?'

'Sam? Sam, where are you?'

'With Gemma,' he said, picking up a note of panic in his brother's voice. 'Why? What's going on? What's the matter?'

'Sam, you have to come. It's Gary—there's been an accident!'

'What! Where? What kind of accident?'

'A car accident. He stole a car, and he's rolled it, and he's trapped underneath, and— Sam, I can smell petrol! You have to come.'

He stabbed a button and put the phone on hands-free. 'Where are you?' he asked, dragging on his jeans while Gemma pulled clothes out of the cupboard and got dressed, handing him his shirt so he could put it on, sorting out his socks and shoes.

'Up at the top of Dunheved Road, near the old mine workings. The car's upside down in a field, and I can hear him screaming!'

'Screaming's good,' Sam said. 'Don't worry, I'm coming. Dial 999 and get police, ambulance and fire brigade there now. I'll be with you in two minutes.' He hung up and turned to Gemma. 'I have to go.'

'I'm coming. You might need help.'

'No, it could be dangerous.'

'Sam, shut up and move,' she said, and ran downstairs after him, her heart in her mouth. No way was she letting Sam put himself in danger without adequate back-up, and, besides, he might need help.

And she'd just have to put her feelings for the boy aside and try and remain professional.

They found the car easily, from the wreckage strewn across the road and Jamie standing by the verge, his face striken.

'Sam, he's here, come on, you've got to get him out!'

'Have you called the emergency services?'

'What? No, Gary said no, he didn't want the police.'

'Don't be ridiculous,' Sam growled. Pulling out his phone, he dialled 999 and ran towards the car, handing the phone to Gemma. 'Keep out of range of the fumes and tell them where we are. I'll give you an update on Gary.' He ducked down beside the car with a sharp grunt, and stuck his head under the edge of the wing. 'Gary? It's Sam. Tell me what hurts.'

'Everything,' the youth sobbed. 'Everything hurts.'

'Can you move?'

'No—I'm stuck, and I can't move at all. It really hurts if I try, but I'm scared and I can't breathe properly.'

'Don't worry, we'll get you out. Are you bleeding anywhere?'

'I don't know. It's wet, but I don't know. And my back's lying on a rock or something, because it really hurts.'

'Sam? Gemma said to give you this,' Jamie said, handing him a torch with shaking hands.

'Great.' But it wasn't, because in the torchlight he could see pink froth around Gary's lips, evidence of lung trauma. And that meant he was running out of time. 'Gemma?'

'Yes?'

He turned his head towards her but toned down the words for Gary's benefit. 'Tell them he's trapped under the car. He's bleeding from a head wound, but his pupils are equal and reactive, and his GCS is 14 at the moment. He's having trouble breathing and he says his back hurts. He could be stuck on a rock. Tell them to get a wriggle on, I think he'd like to get out quite soon.'

'OK,' she called, but he could hear the tremor in her

voice, and he cursed his brother and this stupid, stupid idiot he'd got himself mixed up with. Joy-riding, of all the dangerous and lunatic things, and their timing…

'Right, I'm going to try and get closer and see what's going on,' he said, but he just couldn't. The gap was too small, and every time he tried to shift himself, he got a shaft of pain through his shoulder.

And then Gemma was at his side, handing the phone to Jamie and telling him to give directions and stand by to flag down the emergency services, then tugging at his clothes.

'Sam? Get out of the way, you're too big to fit in there.'

'No way! You aren't going in! Gemz, no!'

'Shut up and move,' she said under her breath. 'Someone needs to assess him, and you can't get in there, and if one of us doesn't he might die.'

'He's not going to die.'

'Do you know that?'

And of course he didn't, but there was a chance they all would, with the petrol leak, and just the thought of Gemma trapped under the car if it went up brought bile to his throat.

'You can't—'

'I can. Please.'

And because she was right, because she was smaller than him, and fitter, and more agile, he had to let her, even though it tore him apart.

He couldn't lose her now—not now, after eleven damn years of wanting her back. Not when they were so close to sorting it out. He felt hot tears sting his eyes, but there was no time for sentiment, and he ran back to his car and pulled his medical bag out of the boot.

'Here, I've got a cannula. See if you can establish

IV access, and I've got some oxygen and a mask.
And, Gemz?'

'Yes?'

'I love you.'

CHAPTER EIGHT

I LOVE YOU.

The words stayed in her head, echoing round and round for the next dreadful minutes as she struggled to get IV access and keep him oxygenated.

'Gary, lie still, you mustn't move your head, you might have a neck injury. Just lie as still as you can for me, that's great, and we'll get you out of here as soon as we can.'

She could hear the sirens approaching, the blue flashing lights flickering on their surroundings and casting weird shadows under the cramped space she was squeezed in with the injured boy. And what she could see in those pulses of light didn't reassure her at all.

She reached her hand under his shoulder and felt something warm and tacky, and her heart sank. Blood. Lots of it, seeping out of him at an unsustainable rate, and he was starting to fit.

'OK, we have to get him out of here *now!*' she yelled, and Sam ducked down behind her and laid his hand on her thigh.

'What's going on?'

'He's fitting, Sam, and there's so much blood— Oh,

hell, he's gone off. He's not breathing. Sam, we have to get the car off him or we don't stand a chance!'

Behind her, she heard Sam relaying her message, then the voices of the other men arguing, and then she felt someone grab hold of her feet and pull her out.

'What are you doing?'

'We're going to roll the car off him. Come on, out of the way, Gemz.'

He hauled her to her feet and they stumbled backwards as the fire crew and policemen heaved in a concerted effort, and the car hovered and then rolled away, bouncing back on its wheels with a series of creaks and groans.

Light flooded the scene, and Sam dived in almost before the car had settled and put his ear to Gary's chest. 'Quiet!' he yelled, and everyone fell silent. 'Right, he's still with us, we need to stabilise his spine and then scoop and run! Move!'

They moved, and in a matter of moments he was log-rolled onto the spinal board, supported and strapped in place and loaded into the waiting ambulance. And Adam Donnelly was there, too, getting into the ambulance and telling Sam to go back to Jamie.

'He needs you, he's in a hell of a state. I've got this one. Maggie's coming, she'll see to him. Right, let's go, everybody!'

Sam turned and looked at Jamie, who was hovering on the fringe, his face ashen and his body shaking. And for the first time he realised there was blood running down his cheek.

He must have scratched himself climbing through the hedge, he thought dumbly, and then Jamie held his stomach and turned away. 'I feel sick,' he said, and retched violently onto the ripped-up grass at the side of the road.

'Jamie?' Gemma crossed to him and put her arm round his shoulders, and Sam stared at him in consternation. Was it just shock? Or…?

'So can anybody tell me how it happened?'

Sam turned to see Lachlan D'Ancey standing in the road with a cluster of police around him, and his heart sank. Of all the things for Jamie to get himself involved in, he thought, and then he heard Jamie talking and his breath jammed in his throat.

'He said he'd borrowed it—I didn't even realise he had a licence, but then I realised it wasn't borrowed at all, and I begged him to stop, but he just went faster, and he was laughing and saying old man Polgrean deserved it if he trashed his car after last night, and then we started to skid and there was a thump and we were just flying through the air.'

Dear God. He'd been in the car?

Sam felt his legs give, and jammed his knees back to stop them collapsing. No! He hadn't been in the car! Surely not? He'd have been injured, and Sam hadn't even so much as glanced at him.

'Jamie, let me see you,' he said, crossing to him and taking the torch from Gemma. He flashed it in his eyes, but to his relief his pupils were equal and reactive and although he was obviously distressed, he was alert.

So he might be concussed, but he wasn't showing signs of brain injury yet. He was lucid, shocked but basically functioning, and Sam lowered the torch and handed it back to Gemma.

'What hurts?' he asked, scanning him quickly and noting he was holding his left arm. 'Were you wearing a seat belt?'

Jamie nodded. 'I was—Gary wasn't.'

Of course not. He'd thought he was immortal, beyond the laws of man or God, but he'd found out the hard way that that simply wasn't true. And he'd taken Jamie with him on that fateful journey with potentially disastrous consequences, and they could have both been dead.

He swallowed hard. 'I need to check you over properly,' he said, wrestling back his control and prioritising.

'Is he dead?' Jamie's voice was hollow, and Sam ached for him. He felt Gemma beside him squeeze his arm, giving him support. 'No, but he's in a very bad way,' he said softly.

'I want to go with him.'

'No, I need to look at you, Jamie. We can go to the surgery.'

'Can we talk to James now? We need to take a formal statement.'

He shook his head. 'Not yet, Lachlan. I want to check him out first. I need to have a proper look at him and X-ray his arm, amongst other things. But you could talk to Mrs Lovelace. She needs to know. Gemma? Keep an eye on him for a minute, I'm just going to pick up my things. I won't be long, bro.'

So while he retrieved his medical equipment from the midst of the wreckage, she put her arm round Jamie's waist and led him to Sam's car and put him into the passenger seat, then perched on the edge and held him tight as he started to shake violently.

'Are you OK, Jamie?' she asked softly.

'I'm fine,' he said, but his voice was flat and his body was shaking like a leaf.

'How's your arm?'

He looked down at it in confusion. 'Um—I don't know. Sore? I can't really feel anything.'

Oh, Sam, come on, she thought. Come and talk to him. Come and check him over.

But then Maggie Donnelly, Adam's wife, appeared and crouched down and asked him a few questions, then went back to Sam, who shook his head. Oh, no, Sam, she thought, because she'd heard Jamie's answers, and she didn't like them.

She went to Sam, taking his hand and gripping it tight. 'They have to take him to hospital, Sam,' she said, backing the paramedic up. 'Maggie's right, they have to get him checked over properly, make sure you haven't missed anything.'

'I can do it.'

'No, Sam, you can't,' she said firmly. 'He's your brother. You're too close. Just go with him and be with him, and I'll go and tell your mother what's happening and wait with her, OK?'

He hesitated for an age, then nodded. 'OK. How will you get back down to town?'

She smiled. 'I'm sure I can convince the patrol car to drop me off.'

He nodded, then, ignoring the onlookers, he bent his head and kissed her. 'Thank you. And thanks for going to Mum. Don't tell her too much.'

She smiled ruefully. 'I won't. Go on, go and look after him. He needs you. He's pretty shaken up. Are you all right to drive?'

He nodded again. It seemed to be all he could do. Words were deserting him and all he could see was the car flying through the air with his brother inside it. He could have been killed, and Gary might already be dead.

'Right, come on, let's go, we'll follow you, but pull over if he deteriorates,' Maggie said, and Sam got into his car beside Jamie, fastened his seat belt for him and then followed the ambulance back to St Piran's.

It was after three before they got home, and Gemma was sitting up with Linda in the kitchen drinking what felt like their hundredth cup of tea as the car pulled up.

'Oh, that's Sam. Gemma, make sure—see if he's brought Jamie.'

Her face crumpled, and Gemma hugged her swiftly and went out of the front door in time to see Jamie unfolding himself stiffly from the front seat, his left arm in a sling and with a back-slab on it, and steristrips on his cheekbone.

'Jamie's here,' she called back, and she heard Linda's sob of relief. She smiled at the young man as he stepped inside, trying not to wince at the rapidly emerging bruises on his face. Linda was going to have a fit. 'Hi, sport, how are you?' she asked gently.

'Sore,' he said, still sounding shaken, 'and I just want to go to sleep but Sam won't let me.'

'You can go to sleep, but I'm going to keep waking you,' Sam warned, 'just to be on the safe side.'

'But I don't want to wake up.'

'I know. Neither do I. But I need to make sure you're all right. You've had a head injury, Jamie, you need to be checked regularly.'

Then Linda was gathering her errant son gently into her arms and sobbing, and Jamie was patting her awkwardly and trying not to cry, and Gemma could see that Sam was struggling, too.

And it had all been so horribly, stupidly unnecessary.

'How's Gary?' she asked Sam in a low voice, and he shrugged.

'Touch and go. Ben Carter filled me in. He's got a shattered pelvis, a flail chest with penetrating rib injuries and a head injury—and that's just the obvious stuff. They're stabilising him, but he's got weak reflexes in his legs and he may have permanent damage to his spinal cord. They're going to scan him when he's stable, but he's on steroids now and they're fighting to keep him alive. The rest will sort itself out if he makes it.'

'Does Jamie know?'

'Yes. He saw him briefly in Resus, but Gary was out of it. He just needed to know he was alive.'

She rubbed his arm comfortingly. 'Sam, I'm so sorry. I'll go now. Call me if there's anything I can do.'

'Sure. Thanks, you're a star.'

He kissed her briefly on the cheek, his hand resting a moment longer on her shoulder, then he turned back to his family to pick up the pieces of yet another crisis.

How much more? How much more could he be asked to take? And how could she even conceivably put any more on him?

She left them to it and went home to bed, only to find the chocolate sauce bowl had been upended in the middle of her bed in all the confusion, and she thought of Sam making love to her, and the conversation they'd been having which had been so violently interrupted— a conversation they had yet to finish.

And she desperately needed to get to bed, but it was trashed, and the spare bed wasn't made up.

Pulling the bedding off, she carried it back downstairs, stuffed the sheet into the washing machine and took the quilt into the sitting room and curled up on the sofa with it snuggled round her. She was cold, she realised, and shaking with reaction now it was all over and there was nothing more to do. She could feel the sobs rising in her chest and she tried to hold them back, but she could still see Gary fitting, the terrible moments as he fought for his young life, and suddenly it was all too much.

'Oh, Sam, I need you,' she sobbed. Cuddling the bedding closer, she buried her face in it, in the scent of Sam's body, and wept for Gary and his family, and the close call Jamie had had, and Sam, struggling to hold it all together—and above all, the senselessness of the illness that had taken her away from him and wasted the last eleven years...

'How are things?'

Sam gave her a weary smile, pushed her backwards into her treatment room and closed the door, then pulled her into his arms and held her without speaking for several minutes.

'Are you OK?' she asked softly, and he nodded, his head moving against her shoulder.

'I'll be fine.'

'And Jamie? I didn't like to ask too much last night, but I've been wondering.'

'He's OK. He's very sore, and he's got some spectacular bruises, but they did an ultrasound aorta scan and X-rayed him all over and—well, he's fine. He's got several fractures in his lower arm and wrist and hand, and his sternum's really bruised from the seat belt, but on the whole he's been incredibly lucky. Unlike Gary.'

She sighed and rubbed his back comfortingly. 'Poor Amanda. Nick's been to see her at the hospital and she's devastated. She said everyone's going to think he's got his just deserts, but she's heartbroken. She's such a sweet woman, but hopelessly ineffectual. According to Nick her husband's a total waste of space, and she keeps letting him back every time he's out of prison. But at least she's got proper contraceptive cover now, so she's not still getting pregnant every time he's out, and maybe the other children will learn by Gary's mistakes and there might be a better chance for them.'

Sam let out his breath on a harsh sigh. 'Maybe. At least he can't hurt anyone else for a while now.'

'No. Amanda said that herself, apparently. Poor woman. Oh, well, if he survives maybe it'll be the making of him.' She straightened up and looked into Sam's red-rimmed, exhausted eyes. 'You don't look as if you had much sleep. What are you doing here? You should be at home in bed. They aren't expecting you.'

'I've brought Jamie in,' he explained. 'He needs another X-ray and a proper cast. Gabriel's just checking him over for me. Could you put the cast on? My left hand's not very useful, I might squeeze it too tight. No feedback.'

'Of course.'

She went down to the X-ray room with him and she and Sam looked at the plates with Gabriel while Jamie sat on the chair and stared blankly at the wall opposite, his battered face expressionless.

'Well, it looks good,' Gabriel said, studying the films on the light box. 'Nothing displaced. See here, a clean break of the radius and ulna, and two of the carpals, here and here, and the scaphoid and first metatarsal both have very fine cracks, but he's been lucky and I think he can have a proper cast now. There's only a little swelling. He'll need the thumb held out to keep the scaphoid aligned, but he should be OK. It'll need another X-ray in two weeks to check the alignment.'

'Great. Thank you, Gabriel. So, Gemma, can you plaster it for him?'

'Sure. Come on, Jamie, let's see what we can do. What colour do you want?'

'I don't care,' he said tonelessly, so she went for dark blue, and swiftly and carefully wrapped his arm in the fibreglass cast, checking it was comfortable and making him wiggle his fingers slightly, then glanced up at Sam. 'Happy with the position?'

'Very. You've done a lovely job, thank you.'

'Thank the time I spent in A and E doing nothing else,' she said, then smiled at Jamie. 'Right, you'll do,' she said, squeezing his shoulder in support. 'Keep it up, rest it and wiggle your fingers every few minutes. And don't get the cast wet, don't stick anything down it if it gets itchy and tell someone if it gets too tight or too loose or if your fingers swell or discolour. OK?'

'I'm fine,' he said, not looking at her, and she could see he was at the end of his rope.

'Take him home, Sam, put him to bed—and get some sleep yourself,' she said softly. 'You both look done in.'

'I can't sleep,' Jamie said. 'I just keep seeing it.'

Sam put an arm gently round his shoulders. 'You'll be all right. Come on, mate, let's go home and see if we can find a DVD.'

She watched them go, and Kate came out of the office and shook her head. 'Poor boy. He must be so upset.'

'He is—I think he feels guilty because he's got away with it so lightly in comparison. I've just been putting a cast on for him to replace the back-slab. Which reminds me, how's Jem's wrist?'

'Oh, he's fine. Back at school and proudly showing

it off to everyone. I think he wishes it had been broken! He's feeling terribly guilty about Digger's paw.'

'He shouldn't. Digger's fine, he's spending all his time on Linda's knee at the moment, and now Jamie's hurt he'll be snuggled up to him as well, so he's got plenty of company while he heals. He'll be spoilt rotten.'

She watched Sam through the glass doors as he put Jamie in the car and then drove away, and she wondered how long it would be before they could spend any time alone together, and when, if ever, they'd finish that long-overdue conversation…

'It's been really odd at school today—quiet. Nobody likes Gary, but they all remember him, and of course the middle brother's still there. It's as if everyone's holding their breath, waiting for the news.'

'Mmm.' Kate nodded at Rob and stirred the teapot thoughtfully. 'Jem said how strange it was without Tel and Tassie. They're above him and Matthew, of course, but he knows Tel.' She didn't let herself dwell on how he'd been so badly bullied by him, but somehow Rob knew that and gave her a gentle one-armed hug.

'He's OK now, Kate.'

'I know. I'm just so glad he's got Matthew for a friend.'

She looked up at him and smiled, and he stared down at her and for a moment she thought—no. Silly. Of course he wasn't going to kiss her. Although if he did…

But he moved away, and she took a deep breath and poured the tea, and the moment was gone. Rob took the tea from her and looked out of the window to where the two boys were playing in the garden.

'Can I ask something?' he asked quietly.

She followed the direction of his eyes and thought, Oh, no. Please, no. 'What?'

'You and Nick…'

He let it hang there in the air, and she looked down into her tea while Rob waited.

Then, when it was obvious she wasn't going to reply, he sighed softly. 'I'm sorry, I shouldn't have brought it up. Forget I said anything.'

She hesitated, then blurted out, 'Nobody knows.'

'Nobody?'

She gave a strangled laugh. 'Oh, Nick knows,' she said, and wondered if her voice sounded as bitter as it felt. 'But hardly anybody else, although that won't last. It's getting more and more obvious as he gets older, and it's only a matter of time.'

She bit her lip, staring at Jem through the window and feeling her heart swell with love. 'It was just once,' she went on. 'A stupid, stupid thing, and I know I ought to regret it, but—I love my son, Rob, and I wouldn't turn the clock back and undo it for anything, because then I wouldn't have him. He would never have existed, and I can't imagine life without him.'

'No. I know what you mean. Losing Annette broke my heart, but I don't think I could ever have dealt with losing Matthew.'

She felt her eyes fill with tears. 'I'm so sorry, Rob. It must have been dreadful.'

'It was—but it's a long time ago now, nearly five years, and I'm ready to move on.'

She looked up at him then, and realised he was talking about her, about them, and she thought, Yes, I'm ready, too. Not for a grand passion, maybe, because there'll always only be Nick, but a gentle love, a caring friend, someone to share things with? I'm ready for that.

'What are you doing on Friday night?' she asked.

'Why?'

'Because the children are both at Alex Pentreath's birthday party, and I wondered if you'd like to come for supper?'

He hesitated for a moment, then smiled. 'That sounds very nice. Thank you. I'd love to.'

'Good,' she said with a smile. 'More tea?'

Gary Lovelace made slight progress in the next few days, and by the end of the week he was downgraded from critical to stable. Not that many of the people in the village cared one way or the other, and not least Mr Polgrean, who was furious about his car and not at all surprised to hear that Jamie had been involved.

And because Jamie was getting better, Sam took him to see the man, to explain that he hadn't been anything to do with its theft and to apologise for all the trouble he'd caused in the past, and after he grudgingly accepted his brother's apology, he turned to Sam and said he owed him one, too.

'This leg business. They said I could have died. You were right, and I had no business bringing up the past like that. If you'd walked away…'

'I could have been struck off for neglect. Let's just forget it and let bygones be bygones, shall we?' he offered, and held out his hand to the crusty old fisherman.

And after an age, he took it, and Sam watched the anger and bitterness drain out of him. He took Jamie home, and the following day he returned to school, to Sam's relief, as he had significant public exams coming up in the next few weeks, and then everything quietened down.

On the home front, at least. Sam was able to go back to work, and it was mayhem, because the tourists were starting to come in larger numbers, especially the surfers, and then Adam Donnelly dropped a bombshell into the mix.

'Maggie and I have decided that the world's a fascinating place and we want to go and see it before we settle down and have a family, so we're going to be leaving Penhally at the end of August,' he announced at their weekly staff meeting.

Amid the exclamations and ripple of comment, Sam wondered what the staffing implications would be—and if Nick would try and talk him into staying on full time.

He wasn't sure, and he certainly didn't know what his answer would be, but that would rather depend on Gemma, he thought, which brought up the subject of the conversation they'd been having when Jamie had phoned him on Monday night.

And it was Friday now, four days later, and he was still no nearer finding out why she'd left him.

But he'd promised to take Jamie over to the hospital this evening to see Gary, and his mother needed his attention, and he would just have to wait. It wasn't the sort of conversation he wanted to rush. There was something she wasn't telling him, something so hugely significant that it had led to the end of their marriage, and he wanted time to talk it through, to get right to the bottom of it and thrash it out, once and for all.

He'd waited nearly eleven years, after all. What difference could a few more days make?

Nick drummed his fingers on the kitchen table and stared blindly out of the window at the dark sea.

He was lonely. Lonely and bored, and he knew Jem was at a party tonight. He glanced at his watch. Ten to ten. Kate might still be up. He could drive past, see if there were any lights on. He wanted to talk to her about Polly Searle—or Polly Carrick, as she now was.

He couldn't remember her at all, but he could remember her father, and he'd been a thoroughly nasty piece of work. No wonder she'd changed her name to her mother's maiden name. He couldn't remember much about her, because he'd not been her GP, of course, Phil had, but Kate would know.

And she was right, they could do with a woman doctor. He hated all the menopause stuff, it was utterly foreign to him and women got so emotional. Yes, a woman doctor would be good.

Tossing his keys in the air and catching them with a sweep of his arm, Nick headed out of the door, locking it behind him out of habit—not that he needed to, probably, with Gary Lovelace out of the frame for now, but old habits died hard.

He drove along Harbour Road past the fishing boats that were all getting ready to go out on the tide, and up Treligga Road to Kate's house. He could see lights on, but as he approached he noticed a strange car on the drive.

Odd. She must have visitors.

And then he saw her cross in front of the kitchen window, and a man—Rob Werrick?—walked into view.

Damn. So he'd been right, they were seeing each other. Unless Rob was picking up something Matthew had left behind? That could be it.

Except, if that was the case, why was Rob looking down at Kate like that? And why…?

Oh, God. He watched in horror as Kate lifted her face to his kiss, then sat, transfixed, as the kiss grew more passionate.

No! But then they moved apart, and he felt a wave of relief, but it was short-lived. The landing light came on, then the bedroom light. And Kate reached up and closed the curtains.

He felt a wave of nausea wash over him and, spinning the wheel, he gunned the car back down the hill and out along the Harbour Road, up past the Smugglers'.

He didn't stop, although he often dropped in for a quiet pint with Tony.

But not tonight. Tonight…

Tonight he just wanted to scream with frustration and bitterness and all the pent-up emotion that was normally locked down tight inside him, and until he had it under control, he was going nowhere.

But he couldn't get the image of Kate and Rob out of his mind, and he was eaten up with a nameless emotion that felt suspiciously like jealousy.

Ridiculous. He didn't even *want* Kate!

But he was damned if he wanted someone else having her, he thought bitterly. He contemplated going home and getting drunk, but dismissed the thought. There was a better way to deal with his frustration, and it was about time he dusted off his social life. Hauling his phone out of his pocket, he scrolled through his numbers, then paused and pressed the call button.

Moments later, it was answered, and he took a breath and leant back, calming himself.

'Louise? It's Nick. How are you? We haven't spoken for a while—I'm sorry, I've been rather tied up. Look, are you busy? I was wondering if I could drop by…'

CHAPTER NINE

'How's Gary?'

'Still in a coma.' Sam sighed and dropped into his chair, and Gemma pushed the door shut and went over and put her arms round him.

'I'm sorry. How's Jamie taking it?'

'He's racked with guilt. Thinks he should have done more to stop him, though God knows what he could have said to make him pay attention, when nobody else has ever succeeded. Even Gertrude Stanbury, our old headmistress, thinks he's probably just a bad person, and she doesn't write people off lightly. She never wrote me off.'

'Because you weren't a bad person, Sam. And neither is Jamie. Even if Mr Polgrean thinks you both are.'

'Oh, not any more,' he said with a chuckle. 'He actually apologised for being rude last Monday, because they'd told him how close he'd got to losing his leg, and he realised that if I'd listened to him and walked off, he might have lost it. Or worse. And he even accepted Jamie's apology for getting mixed up with Gary, so it was pretty cosy all round, really.'

'Good grief, wonders will never cease,' she said with a chuckle. 'And your mum?'

'Oh, she's all right, I suppose, but still a bit shocked and she's struggling to get over her own problems, but Lauren's been great with her and she's doing all right. Her hand's still a bit weak and her legs are a little unsteady, but fundamentally she's fantastic, considering.'

'And the dog?'

'He's getting along.'

'Good.'

Gemma perched on the edge of the desk facing him, and ran her finger over his knee thoughtfully.

'So—does that mean you're able to get out a bit more now?'

He raised a brow, the smile he couldn't quite prevent playing around his mouth.

'Well, that very much depends, of course, on what's on offer.'

'On offer? I was rather thinking it might be your turn to do the offering.'

He sat up slowly, leaning forwards and reaching up to pull her down onto his lap. 'Well, now, let me think. How about dinner somewhere? Not the Smugglers'. Somewhere a bit more private, where we aren't going to run into whoever's acting as Town Crier this week. Somewhere like Padstow, or Rock?'

She cocked her head on one side. 'That sounds rather posh.'

A little frown crossed his brow, and he gave her a quizzical smile. 'Maybe it's time I took you out and spoiled you a little.' And then afterwards, when he'd wined and dined her, he could take her back to her house and talk to her, get her to open up to him, tell him whatever it was that had torn them apart. 'Perhaps Friday?'

'Maybe,' she said, but she hesitated. There was so much he didn't know, so much she still had to tell him, and until it was out in the open, she really didn't want to get into the whole formal dinner thing. It just seemed wrong, and she didn't know how she could sit there and pretend that everything was all right.

'How about coming round to mine for supper in the meantime?' she suggested. 'And maybe this time we'll get to finish our meal.'

And that all-important conversation.

'That would be good. My sister Beth's coming over this evening with her brood to see Jamie and Mum, but I could do tomorrow or Wednesday.'

'Make it Wednesday,' she said, suddenly wanting to stall this whole thing and wishing she'd never brought it up. 'Seven-thirty? I've got a clinic before, so I can't get away too early.'

'Seven-thirty's fine,' he said, and then patted her on the bottom. 'Come on, off my lap, gorgeous, before I get too distracted to work. I've got a rammed surgery this morning, and a load of visits, and that's before the phone line's been open for more than five minutes!'

He was right, it was a hectic day, and Tuesday was no better.

By Wednesday she'd managed to work herself up into a frenzy about their meal—well, more specifically the conversation after it—and the last thing she wanted at a busy well-woman clinic was children running around. Not with what she was going to have to tell Sam later, anyway. And there were three of them, the

O'Grady children—although one wasn't running anywhere, and she frowned at him.

Liam. She knew him—and he was normally as lively as a cricket. He must be going down with something, she thought, and then dismissed it as she worked her way through her list of patients.

Until she got to the last, Siobhan O'Grady and her little brood, and then as she ushered the children in, Gemma glanced down at Liam and frowned again. He had bruises on his arm, big bruises, like finger marks, and she thought, No, not Siobhan. She was a wonderful mother. And the father was a nice man, a policeman. So what…?

'Hello, Liam,' she said, crouching down beside him. 'You're very quiet today, you're normally tearing around. Aren't you feeling well?'

He shook his head, and Siobhan said worriedly, 'No, I don't think he can be, he's been so quiet, you know, and he's not the quietest child. And he's so pale. I thought, if it went on much longer, I ought to bring him to the doctor and have him checked out, but perhaps you could have a look at him since he's here with me now, just in case he's picked something up at school.'

'Of course, you're at school now! What a big boy. Can I have a look at you, Liam? Want to pop up here?'

And she lifted him carefully to the couch and sat him on the edge and studied him. And her heart began to pound slowly. 'How long has he had the bruises?'

'Oh, I hadn't even seen them! Good grief, there're dreadful! Niall, what have you been doing to your brother?'

'Nothing! I didn't do nothing, I swear!'

But alarm bells were ringing, and Gemma lifted

trembling fingers and felt the sides of Liam's neck. Peas. Chains of peas, running down each side, and under his chin, and in his armpits.

'I think we need to get a doctor to have a look at you, my little fellow,' she said, lifting him down and putting him carefully onto a chair. 'Siobhan, stay here with them, I'll be back in a moment.'

And she went out of the door, closed it behind her and took a long, steadying breath. Thank heavens there was nobody in the waiting room, because she was shaking like a leaf, her heart was racing and she thought at any moment she might be sick.

Her legs wobbling, she walked down the stairs and over to Reception. 'Is there a doctor free?'

'No—oh, yes, someone's just come out of Sam's consulting room. Nip in now, quickly,' Hazel said, and she thought, of all the doctors, but maybe he was the right one, and maybe this would open the gates to that conversation.

She tapped on the door and went in, and he glanced up and his eyes softened and he smiled at her. 'Hello, my gorgeous girl. What can I do for you—? Gemma? Are you all right? What is it?' He got up and crossed over to her, a frown pleating his brow, and she forced herself to smile.

'It's not me.' Not this time. 'It's a little boy upstairs— Liam O'Grady. He's tired, pale, listless, his glands are up.' She swallowed. 'And he's bruising.'

Sam frowned and tilted his head to one side. 'Leukaemia?'

'I think so.'

'Oh, hell. Right. Who's with him?'

'His mother, and his brother and baby sister.'

'Is there a father?'

'Yes. He's a policeman. He'll be at work—he's in the CID.'

'OK. I'll come up. They'll have to take him straight over to St Piran for blood tests, if you're right, and then they'll let them know in the next day or so, I guess.'

Or sooner...

'Has she got a car?'

'Yes. She lives up near me, I see her quite often.'

'Right, let's go and have a look at him—Liam, did you say?'

'Yes.'

And she led the way back up, hoping she was wrong, hoping that Sam would tell her she was imagining it, that this dear, delightful little boy wouldn't have to go through the hell of—

'Siobhan, this is Dr Cavendish.'

'Sam! Oh, I'm so pleased it's you!' Siobhan said, her eyes filling.

He smiled warmly. 'Hello, Siobhan. Long time no see. We were in the same year at school,' he explained to Gemma. 'So, which of these little men is Liam?'

'He is,' Niall said, and Sam, having already zeroed in on Liam, nodded and crouched down beside his chair.

'Hello, Liam. I'm Dr Sam. I'm an old friend of your mummy's. Can I have a look at you, do you think?' And at Liam's nod, he lifted him onto the couch, laid him down and gave him a gentle but thorough examination. And then he pulled the T-shirt down over his skinny little chest, straightened up and met Siobhan's worried eyes.

'It's serious, isn't it?' she whispered. 'Holy Mother of God, Sam, tell me it's not serious.'

'Gemma, have we got any toys?'

'Of course. I'll just…' She stuck her head round the other treatment-room door, where Lara had just finished her clinic. 'Lara? I wonder, would you mind playing with the children for a moment? They're a bit bored in here.'

'I'm sure I've got lots of toys. Shall we go and have a look?' And Lara smiled at the children, scooped Liam up gently and held her hand out to little Caitlin.

And as the door shut behind them, Siobhan started to shake uncontrollably. 'So—come on, Sam, for the love of God tell me!'

'He's going to have to have some blood tests, and then the haematologist will talk to you, but, yes, I'm afraid it may well be serious, Siobhan. I'm very sorry.'

'But…' Her eyes swivelled to Gemma's, desperately seeking reassurance. 'No. Tell me—tell me it's not leukaemia.'

So she had known, or suspected. Oh, dear help her, poor woman, Gemma thought with a detached part of her brain, because the rest of her was screaming in denial and just wanted to run away, as far and as fast as she could.

'I'm sorry, but it's the most probable cause of his symptoms. They'll take blood, and as soon as they have the results, which is usually within hours, they'll do a bone-marrow biopsy if it's indicated, and then if that confirms it they'll start chemotherapy straight away, possibly tomorrow.'

'Tomorrow!' she gasped, sagging into a chair and staring at Gemma open-mouthed. 'No! They can't! My baby!'

'Siobhan, it may not be. They have to test for it, but—'

'But you know, don't you? You know. Oh, God, I want Sean. Can I call him now?'

'Of course you can,' Sam said, but she couldn't hold her phone, far less speak, so Sam took it from her and asked her husband to come down to the surgery, while Gemma sat beside her and held her hands and waited.

And then, because he'd only been at the other end of Harbour Road, Sean was dropped off by the patrol car he'd been in and was shown up to the room, and Siobhan threw herself sobbing into his arms and Sam filled him in on what they suspected.

'So—what's the prognosis?' Sean asked directly, meeting Sam's eyes head on, and Sam shrugged.

'I can't tell you. We don't even know if it is leukaemia. We do know that it's a classic presentation, but that's all. He will have to have the blood test to be sure, and the bone marrow biopsy to confirm it and to indicate the best treatment, and only then will you have any idea—but treatment is better than it's ever been, and children do survive this in great numbers. But you have to have it confirmed, and until then, there's no point in torturing yourselves.'

Out of the corner of his eye Sam saw Gemma shake her head slightly, as if to clear it, and then he looked more closely. She was chalky grey, her fists were clenched and her knuckles white, and she was shaking. All over.

'Gemma?'

She jerked to her feet. 'I'll go and see how the children are. You take as long as you need. We'll be next door.'

She went out, closing the door behind her with trembling fingers, and then took a moment to breathe in deeply before following the sound of giggling. She dredged up a smile. 'Hello, all. How are you doing?'

'What's wrong with Mummy?' Liam asked, and she crouched down beside him and swallowed hard.

'Nothing, sweetheart. She just needed to talk to the doctor, and we thought it would be boring for you all.'

'Is it because I'm sick?'

Oh, hell. But experience had taught her that honesty was the best policy, and age was no barrier to understanding. It was just a case of pitching it right, and she had no idea if she would. But she had to answer him, because he was waiting, and so she nodded slowly. 'Yes. She's worried, but she would be. You're her big boy, and you aren't feeling well, and she wants you to be better.'

'So will I have to have medicine?'

She nodded. 'I think so. The first thing is you'll need to go to the hospital and they'll need to take a little bit of blood from you.'

'With a needle?' he asked, his eyes wide, and she remembered that Liam hated needles. Passionately. His pre-school booster had been a work of art to get into him, and had taken her weeks of patient persuasion.

'Yes,' she said, because there was no point in lying. 'Yes, there will be a needle, but they'll be very gentle.'

'No! I don't want to go to the hospital! I want you to do it here!'

And then Sam was sticking his head round the door and frowning. 'Everything all right?'

'Liam wants me to take his blood.'

The frown grew deeper. 'How?'

How what? How would she do it? Or how did Liam know? How had she been so stupid as to tell him?

'He asked if he would have to have medicine, and so I told him the truth,' she said simply, and after a moment, Sam nodded.

'OK. I'll ring the hospital. It might be possible for you to do that. I'll ask.'

'No, let me. I'll know what bottles we have and if we can do it. Liam, stay here with Lara and Caitlin and Niall, and I'll be back in a moment, OK?'

He shook his head. 'I want to come.'

She looked at Sam, and he shrugged, as much as to say, Well, it's his illness, and you know him. Your call.

'Come on, then,' she said, holding out her hand, and when they were back in the other room, he went straight to his mother and climbed on her knee and sat there, watching Gemma as she explained what she'd told him.

'But, Liam, you have to realise that if I take your blood today and they say you need to go to hospital for your medicine, you'll have to go. I can't do it here. So although I may be able do this first bit, I can't do any more. You do understand that, don't you? It's not that I don't want to, it's just that they have special people to do it, and they're very good. They have lots of children there, and they know how to do it so it doesn't hurt and they can look after you.'

His chin wobbled a bit, but then he nodded.

'OK, let's ring them,' she said, and dialled the hospital number and asked for Jo in Haematology, while Sam watched her thoughtfully.

'Hi, it's Gemma Johnson at Penhally Bay Surgery—hi, Jo. No, I know. It's about a patient this time,' she said, and he thought, What an odd remark, as if she knew the person on the other end and talked to them about other things. What other things? Maybe she'd

had some training there or knew them socially.
Whatever, she was still talking, and the part of him that
wasn't trying to work out the sub-text was listening.

'We have a child with suspected ALL—can I do the
bloods here? He's needle phobic and we've been working together on this, so he wants me to do it. No, they
can bring them up straight away. OK, tell me what I'll
need, and I can do that.'

She scribbled down the tests that would be required,
and the tubes she'd need, then thanked Jo and hung up,
then smiled at Liam. And if you didn't know her well,
she looked fine now, he thought, except for something
in her eyes, some shadow that haunted them. But what?
What was going on here?

'OK, Liam, I can do it here, so do you want to lie
down or stay on Mummy's lap?'

'Mummy,' he mumbled round his thumb, snuggling
closer, and Sam could see his eyes beginning to fill.

Oh, hell, so were his. He blinked hard and concentrated on Gemma, ready to step in if she needed help,
but she seemed to be managing fine. More than fine.
Except for the look in her eyes.

'Right. I'm going to put a little strap round your arm
to stop all the blood in it from disappearing back into
your body and running away from me, and then I can find
a tiny little vein and get some out. Here, pull this end and
stick it on there—no, bit tighter—that's lovely. Oh, yes,
look, here's a lovely little vein. I'll put some special
magic jelly on it like we did before, and then it won't hurt
a bit. Now, do you know what colour your blood's going
to be when it comes out?' she asked, and he nodded.

'Red,' he said. 'Timmy had a nosebleed in the play-
ground last week and it was bright red.'

'Well, that's a funny thing, because when it comes out and hits the air, it changes to bright red, but when it's in your arm, it's actually quite dark, almost purple.'

'Purple?' he said, giggling. 'No, it's not purple!'

'Shall we see? I tell you what, shall we ask Mummy to hold your hand out here for me, so I can see better? That's lovely, Siobhan, just hold it straight on your arm like that. Fantastic. Right—red or purple?'

'Red!'

And with a chuckle, she slid the needle in, clipped the first bottle on and they watched it fill.

'It *is* purple!' Liam said. 'I thought it would be red!'

'I wonder what colour the next one will be?' she asked, swapping bottles, and in the end she had several, and to Liam's disappointment not one of them was red.

'But,' she said, pressing a swab over his vein as she drew the needle out, 'when we take this swab off in a minute, I bet you the blood on it's red.'

'Wow. That's really odd,' Liam said, resting back against his mother and watching as Gemma wrote his name on all the labels.

'OK, you need to take these in straight away, and go to the haematology lab and ask for Jo. She's expecting you. And they'll process them immediately.' She ruffled Liam's hair. 'Well done, sport. You're a good boy. And don't worry, they'll look after you.'

'What about Niall and Caitlin?' Sean asked, and she could see he was pale and hanging on to his control by a thread.

'Is there someone you can leave them with for now?'

'My mother—we'll drop them round there on our way. I'll ring her from the car. Gemma, thank you so much.'

Siobhan broke off, and Gemma bent and hugged them both, mother and son, then said, 'Right—what colour is the swab?'

And lifting it away to replace it with a little plaster, she showed it to Liam.

'It's red!' he said. 'So I *was* right!'

'Yes, we both were. Clever, eh? Now, you need to keep your finger on that for a while to make sure the bleeding's stopped, OK? Good boy. Right, here are the bottles,' she said, handing the plastic bags to Sean. 'Let us know.'

'We will,' Sean promised, and he ushered his family out, with Sam following, while she sank down into her chair and closed her eyes.

She felt drained, exhausted, and her mind was whirling, dragging her back down into the vortex, and she had to get out of here. Had to escape, to run away, to forget the awfulness, the fear, the terrible loneliness of that dreadful journey that Liam and his family were about to make.

A journey she knew all too well…

What the hell was going on with Gemma?

Sam wanted to go back up, to see her, to get to the bottom of it, but his patients were backed up wall to wall, and when he rang her room, there was no reply. Damn. And he couldn't see the car park from his surgery, so he had no idea if she'd left the building, but—she'd said she had a late surgery tonight, and he was going round for a meal at seven-thirty, so she should be here.

Maybe she'd taken Lara's room? Or gone to the loo, or made herself a cup of tea. The waiting room upstairs had been empty, he remembered, and told himself not to worry. There were other things demanding his attention, and he could think about her later.

Except he couldn't get her out of his mind, and he kept replaying the scene with Liam over and over in his head. She'd been so good with him, and she'd known so much about it. Almost too much. As if…

Cold dread washed over him as the thought crystallised. No. It couldn't have been her, but maybe a member of her family had suffered from it—perhaps a sibling who'd died? But he knew she only had one brother, and she hadn't mentioned it, and he was sure—absolutely sure—that she would have done.

Unless…

Oh, God. His heart began to pound, and his palms felt damp. Not Gemma. Surely she would have told him? Surely…

But there was a scar on her chest. Just a tiny scar, to the side of her sternum, high up below her collar bone. He'd noticed it last week, when he'd been making love to her, licking chocolate off her soft, pale skin. And he'd seen it, felt it, a tiny hard bump in the skin. The sort of scar that would be left by a central line during treatment for leukaemia.

He stood up and went over to the window, staring out across the headland at the side, past the building work which was still in progress, but he didn't see anything except the scar, and the look in her eyes as she'd taken Liam's blood and comforted his parents and calmly told them what to expect.

Because she knew, he realised, every inch of the road they'd have to travel. She'd taken every step, walked every mile of it—and she'd done it alone, without him.

But when? Surely not then? Surely that wasn't why? She hadn't been ill—had she?

He cast his mind back, trying to pick up clues from their time together that summer, but he could only remember the good times. The laughter, the loving, long into the night, so that the next day he could hardly wake her.

Because she'd been so tired.

And he'd chased her up the beach and back to the house, laughing and giggling, and she'd turned just as she'd been going in and she'd missed the step and hit her shin, and she'd come up with a hell of a bruise.

She'd hit it hard, but—that hard? Hard enough to turn her shin black? It only took one little vessel to rupture, but what if it had been more than that? And she'd had a niggling cough, too—a cold that seemed to linger. She'd been working hard for her A levels, and she'd said she was run down, but it just didn't clear.

He went back to his desk, logged into his computer and found her patient file. He could look it up—scroll through it and get the answers, but he wanted to hear it from her and, anyway, he knew.

He logged off again and squeezed his eyes shut, the certainty devastating him.

She'd had leukaemia—his dear, darling, precious Gemz had had leukaemia, and instead of telling him, she'd shut him out, let her parents whisk her away, and all she'd left him was a note.

How could she?

How could she have done that, excluded him, when he loved her so much he would have died for her.

He sprang up again, shoving his chair back so hard it hit the wall, and picking up his jacket he headed for the door.

'Where's Gemma?'

Kate was behind the desk looking for something in the filing cabinet, and she hesitated at his sharp tone.

'She's gone.'

'Gone where?'

'I don't know. Home, I suppose. She said she wasn't feeling well. Lara's covering her clinic. Did you want a nurse for something?'

'No. It doesn't matter. Can you ask Hazel to reschedule the rest of my patients, please? I have to go.'

'Of course—Sam? It's not Jamie, is it? Is everything all right?'

No, it bloody well wasn't all right, it was about as wrong as it could get, but he wasn't talking about it with her, or with anybody but his wife.

'It's fine,' he said, and shoving the door out of the way, he limped out into the car park, got in his car and drove to her house.

CHAPTER TEN

SAM pulled up outside Gemma's house and sat there, unable to move.

He felt sick, his heart racing, grief and anger and bitterness churning through him violently so that he wasn't sure if he could even talk to her. Not now. Not like this.

But she was there, standing at her door watching him, and he could see it in her face.

So he got out of the car and walked up to her door, and without a word she stood back and let him in. He could see tearstains on her cheeks, and her eyes were red-rimmed, but sympathy was a long way down his list of boiling emotions at that moment and so he ignored it and walked through the house and out onto the deck at the back.

He couldn't sit inside tidily on a chair while they had this conversation, because frankly he just didn't trust himself at the moment and he needed air, needed space. He heard her footsteps behind him, and turned to her, needing to see her face while she made this explanation.

And it had better be damned good.

'You had it, didn't you? That's why you left. Because you had leukaemia,' he said, making himself say the words although they threatened to choke him.

Her eyes wavered, but held his, and he could see the tears welling again. 'Yes.'

'Why? Why did you leave me? For God's sake, Gemma, we were *married*! I'd promised to stand by you, to be there for you, but you didn't give me the chance! You just walked away, without explaining, without talking to me about it, and you left me hanging there in free space, with no clues as to why you'd gone, what I'd done wrong. Do you have any idea—*any* idea at *all*—of what that felt like? I loved you so much. I'd promised to be with you through thick and thin, and you couldn't even tell me when something was wrong.'

'Because I didn't want to stop you doing all the things you were going to do, Sam!' she said, and he could see the tears streaming down her face. 'You were nineteen, for heaven's sake! Nineteen! You had your whole life ahead of you, and I couldn't hold you back. I didn't have the right to hold you back.'

'Oh, you did. I gave you that right, Gemz—I gave you that right when I married you, for better, for worse, in sickness and in health. And I meant it, every last damned word I said to you. And you didn't give me the chance—'

He broke off and turned away, and then he felt Gemma's hand on his arm.

'Sam? I did it for you.'

'Well, you had no right!' he roared, turning on her with all the anger and frustration and hurt of the last eleven years spewing out of him in a hideous tide that threatened to destroy him. 'You had no right to do that on my behalf! It wasn't your decision! It was mine, and you took it away from me and you took away the only thing that mattered to me, the only thing I cared about, the only decent thing that had ever happened to me in my whole life! And I can never, ever forgive you for that.'

And pushing her aside, he strode out, ignoring the pain in his ankle as he ran down the steps to his car and got in, slamming the door and driving off with a squeal of tyres.

He didn't know where he was going, but he found himself at the beach—not the little cove where they'd shared their love with such innocence and passion. He couldn't go there, it would hurt too much, but he needed to hear the sea, to have the crash of the waves drown out the screaming pain in his heart.

He stumbled out of the car and down the steps to the sand, walking unseeing past the few people still there on the beach, down to the far end. And he sat on a rock above the water and tried to breathe, tried to slow his heart and let his feelings settle, let the grief and anger and betrayal die down to a level he could deal with before it destroyed him...

'Gemma?'

She heard the knock on the door, heard the woman's voice and got numbly to her feet.

Siobhan O'Grady was standing on the step, her tear-stained face pleading, and Gemma held out her arms as the woman fell into them, sobbing.

'Oh, Siobhan, come in,' she said gently, and led her through to the sitting room. Not the deck. She couldn't sit out there where Sam had...

'Tell me. What did they say?'

'He's got to have a bone-marrow thing in the morning to confirm it, but they think it's ALL—is that right?'

She nodded. 'Acute lymphoblastic leukaemia. It's the most common in children and young people. And it can be treated, Siobhan.'

She nodded. 'So—why do they look at the bone marrow? If it's a blood thing?'

'Because the bone marrow makes the blood cells. And in ALL, the white blood cells or lymphoblasts which have gone wrong don't work properly to mop up infections, which is why children are often run down and unwell. And they often have fewer red blood cells and platelets, which means they have symptoms of anaemia and difficulty clotting, hence the bruising.'

'So—what happens now? Oh, God, Gemma, I can't stand it, my poor baby…'

Gemma hugged her close and let her cry while her own heart was breaking, and after a while Siobhan pulled herself together and straightened up. 'I'm sorry, but I can't cry on Sean, he's falling apart, and so's Mum, and I just needed to talk to someone who knew what I was talking about.'

Oh, she knew. She knew only too well, but that was fine. Talking to Siobhan didn't hurt her, but talking to Sam…

She needed to talk to Sam, but not now. He needed time to calm down, time to think. And Siobhan needed her.

'Now they do the bone-marrow aspiration, and then they go from there, working out a treatment schedule, but he won't be in hospital all that time. He'll come backwards and forwards, spending a lot of time at home between cycles, and you'll get a great deal of support from the hospital and from the surgery, but you just have to take it one day at a time, Siobhan. And you will get there.'

'Oh, dear lord, I hope so, but I don't know how to be strong for them,' she murmured, and Gemma held out a box of tissues to her.

'You'll be fine. At least it's all under way now, and you just have to be strong for Liam. It'll be hard for him, and you have to help him, but it'll be hard for you, too, and you have to look after each other, and the other two children. I know it's difficult, but don't forget about them, and don't suffocate them. And lean on Sean, and encourage him to talk, because men are bad at that. And if you ever need to talk, I'm always here, and I'll always have time for you.'

'You're so kind. Thank you.'

'It's no problem.'

'I have to get back,' she said, standing up and mopping her nose again. 'I've got to do some washing for Liam, and I haven't even thought about feeding us—I've fed the children and put them to bed, but somehow, food…'

'You have to eat. Go on, go home and look after yourself, because you have to stay well for them all. And good luck tomorrow. Keep me in touch, won't you?'

'Oh, I will, thank you Gemma,' she said, and, giving her one last hug, she went down the steps and hurried back to her house, leaving Gemma to her tumbling thoughts.

She went back out to the deck, and sat down on a chair and waited. Would Sam come back, or did she need to go and find him?

What if he didn't come back? she thought suddenly, on a wave of dread. What if he left again, went off back to Africa? He'd said he couldn't forgive her. What if he'd meant it—really meant it, meant he couldn't, wouldn't forgive her, and so it was all over, back to square one, only this time it was his idea and not hers? The pain swamped her, even the thought was agonising, and she felt a sob jam in her throat, trapped there by the rising tide of panic.

She had to find him. Had to go and look for him and change his mind, but where?

The beach, she thought. Their beach.

And she grabbed her keys, slammed the door shut behind her and ran down the steps to her car. She knew exactly where to find him—but he wasn't there. And he wasn't at his house, and she drove round for ages, looking blindly through her tears for his car, but it was nowhere to be seen, and finally she had to admit that he might have gone, that it could be too late.

That maybe at last their marriage was finally at an end.

With the last shreds of her control, she pulled over to the side of the road, cut the engine and began to sob.

'Sam?'

He lifted his head and stared blankly at the French doctor.

'Gabriel—hi. Sorry, I was miles away.'

'So I could see. No dog today?'

'No, I—uh—I haven't been home.'

'Mind if I join you?'

Why the hell would he want to join him? But it was a public place, and he could hardly tell him to leave.

'Sure.'

Gabriel sat down on another rock, the slender grey-hound leaning against his leg, and he idly pulled the dog's ears and gazed out to sea.

'I often come here when things seem—confused,' he said quietly. 'I listen to the gulls, and the sound of the water, and things straighten out a little bit.'

Sam grunted. Nothing was straightening out for him, that was for sure. He was as confused and hurt and bitter as before, and it would take more than a few seagulls to sort him this time.

'I saw your patients this evening, by the way.'

Sam sighed. 'Thanks. I'm sorry, I just had to get away.'

'Want to talk about it?'

'Not really. There's nothing you can do, nothing anyone can do. She made her choices years ago.'

'Are we talking about Gemma here?'

He sighed quietly, then nodded. 'You know, we were married, Gabriel. I was nineteen, she was eighteen, and I loved her so much it hurt. And I thought she loved me, so I married her—and then she found out she had leukaemia, and without telling me she just walked away. She just walked away, and she left me a note, for God's sake! She didn't even have the guts to talk to me, and I only found out today by accident.'

Gabriel made a soft sound of sympathy. 'You know, *mon ami*, maybe she did have guts. Maybe she was misguided, but maybe she did what she did for you.'

Sam grunted. 'That's what she said, but she had no right to make that choice for me.'

'Of course not. Lauren did the same for me. When she found out she was going blind, she tried to cut me out of her life, and gradually I worked out what she was doing—but at least I knew she had something wrong, and I bullied it out of Oliver, and then I confronted her with it. I asked her, if it had been me, would she have left me to cope alone, and she was furious. Of course not! But she asked this of me, to leave her to cope alone because she didn't want to be a burden to me. As if the woman I love more than life itself could ever be a burden.'

Sam felt hot tears scald his eyes, and turned away. 'I'm just so angry with her.'

'Of course. I was angry with Lauren. But you love her, *non*?'

'Oh, yes. I've loved her for ever. I've never stopped loving her.' His voice broke, and he felt Gabriel's hard, warm hand on his knee.

'Then go and talk to her, Sam. Tell her how you feel, forgive her. And don't waste any more of your lives apart. It's so obvious you belong together. Don't let one mistake be responsible for any more.'

And getting to his feet, Gabriel walked away, Foxy trotting quietly beside him, leaving Sam alone with the seagulls.

She wasn't there.

Her car was gone, and she wasn't there. And he had no idea where to start looking, so he sat there on her step and waited, his thoughts in turmoil. And finally, as the sun set, she appeared, turning into her little parking place and cutting the lights on her car.

She got out slowly and walked up to him, and he stood up stiffly and held out his hand to her, his heart contracting at the sight of her ravaged face.

'I'm sorry. I shouldn't have yelled at you. Can we try again?'

'Oh, Sam—I thought you'd gone,' she said, and fell into his arms, sobbing, just as Siobhan had fallen into hers. She fumbled for her keys and he took them and let them in, then shut the door and pulled her back into his arms.

'I love you,' he said brokenly, desperate to sort this out, knowing that he had to be with her, that he had to hear her side of it and learn to forgive her, because nothing else would be right. 'I've always loved you, and I can't walk away from you now. But we have to talk.'

'I know. Sam, I'm so sorry.'

He held her close, rocking her, and gradually her tears slowed and she eased away. 'Come in to the sitting room,' she said, and he picked up the soggy tissues and raised a brow.

'Siobhan,' she explained, taking them from him and binning them. 'She came to say they're doing the bone-marrow aspiration tomorrow, and she just needed to lean on someone.'

'And she chose you, of all people.'

'But at least I *know*, Sam. I know what it's like.'

'Tell me,' he said softly, pulling her down beside him, and she went into his arms and snuggled closer, loving the smell of sea air and soap and Sam that drifted to her nostrils, needing the strength of his arms around her while she did this, because to talk about it brought it all back, and it had been the most traumatic and terrifying and desperate time of her life, and she'd needed him so badly.

'What do you want to know?' she asked, steeling herself.

'Everything. Everything that happened, from start to finish.'

She nodded, took a deep breath and began with the facts. 'OK. It was the Monday after we got married on the Thursday. My parents had come down on Saturday afternoon and found us, and I hadn't talked to them, but I thought on the Monday when you went back to work that I ought to try and make peace with them, tell them how much I loved you, why I'd married you—but when I got up, I felt terrible. My leg was covered in bruises from when I'd fallen up the steps, but I noticed others that morning, ones I hadn't got a clue about. I'd put it down to—well, to all the love-making,' she said, feeling herself colour.

His breath sucked in. 'Was I so rough you thought I'd given you bruises?' he asked, sounding so appalled that she laughed a little unsteadily and lifted her hand to his taut, stubbled jaw, cradling it.

'No, of course not,' she murmured as he turned his face into her hand and pressed his lips to her palm. 'You were always gentle with me. That was why I couldn't understand it. But then I thought about the cough that wouldn't go, and I'd had a headache all Sunday and I was so tired all the time. Again, I thought, because of being awake at night, but we'd dozed all day, too, so it was silly. I thought it might be because I was so upset about my parents, but when I went to see them my mother took one look at me and burst into tears and told me I looked dreadful, and it was the first time I'd looked in the mirror for days, and I was chalk white under my tan, and I had black circles, and I knew then that it was more than that, that something must be dreadfully wrong.'

'Was that when you went home to Bath?'

She shook her head. 'No. No, that was later, after…' She trailed off, and felt his arms tighten around her in silent support.

'Later?'

'My parents took me straight to see Phil Tremayne, Nick's brother, and insisted he see me immediately. He took one look at me and sent me straight to the hospital.'

'On the Monday morning.'

'Yes. We got there—oh, I suppose it was about ten-thirty? And they did the bloods and asked me to wait, and then the consultant haematologist called us into his room and told me he wanted to do a bone-marrow biopsy because he thought I had leukaemia.'

She felt the tension in him ratchet up a notch. 'And?'

She closed her eyes, but she could still see everything—her parents' faces, the kind, professional sympathy of the haematologist, the room where they took her for the bone-marrow aspiration.

'He did it straight away,' she said, oblivious to the tears that were trickling down her cheeks, 'and by three I had my diagnosis—acute lymphoblastic leukaemia. And the treatment was going to take months, so obviously we couldn't stay in Cornwall, because my father would have to go back to work and, anyway, Bath has a brilliant treatment unit, so they packed everything up into the car, and I wrote you the note,' she said, trying hard to hold it together because writing that letter had been the hardest thing she'd had to do at that, oh, so difficult time, 'and we dropped it into the beach house on the way home.'

'But—why?' he asked, his voice cracking. 'Why didn't you find me and tell me? I would have come with you. Why shut me out, Gemz? I needed to be with you, I would have stood by you, come with you to the hospital, held your hand, stayed at your bedside.'

'Of course you would,' she said sadly, hating the anguish in his voice and wondering even now if she'd do the same thing all over again, for him. 'But you wouldn't have gone to uni, and you would have sacrificed your chances of a medical career for me, and I couldn't let you do that. I loved you too much to take that away from you.'

He shook his head. 'We could have worked it out. I could have gone to uni in Bristol, just as I did, and visited you every day. I came to see you—did you know? Your parents told me you didn't want to see me, and they turned me away.'

She nodded miserably. 'I told them to.'

He stiffened and turned his head so she could see his eyes. 'What? You were there?'

She nodded again. 'In the sitting room. I saw you outside, and I wanted you so badly, Sam,' she said, unable to hold back the tears. 'I wanted you to hold me, to tell me it was all going to be all right, but it wouldn't have been fair, and I looked so awful—I'd lost my hair again, and I was so thin, and I was feeling really sick, and I knew if you saw me you'd be angry with me for not telling you, and I couldn't cope with it.'

'No,' he breathed raggedly, folding her against his heart. 'Oh, no, my love, no. I would have held you. I wouldn't have cared about your hair, or how thin you were or how awful you looked, and I wouldn't have been angry.'

'You were today.'

He sighed and closed his eyes. 'I know. But that was different. Today I was angry because you'd taken away that choice from me, the choice I'd already made to be with you, to support you when things went wrong. But back then—Gemz, I made those vows meaning them, and I would have stood by you. It was a real commitment, and it didn't matter that I was only young. I meant every word, and I meant it for ever.'

'Did you? Or was it only because you wanted to

sleep with me and I wouldn't let you if we weren't married?'

He exhaled sharply. 'Is that what you thought? That I married you for sex?' he asked, his voice horrified. 'Dear God, Gemma—sex doesn't matter that much.'

'It does if you're nineteen and impulsive. I thought it was just a spur-of-the-moment thing, a crazy idea. I thought you'd get over me. I really thought you would, that it had probably only been about sex—well at least, for you.'

He shook his head emphatically. 'No! If I'd wanted sex, I'd have found it somewhere. But I'd already waited a year for you. All that last year, from the moment I met you, there was no one else—and there hasn't been, in all this time. No one. Because you're the only woman I want…'

His voice cracked again, and he rested his head against hers and dragged in a breath. 'So what happened after the bone-marrow aspiration?'

'We went back to Bath, and I was admitted the following morning. I had four cycles of chemo, over the next five months. I was meant to have five, but they couldn't give me the last one because my immune system was so knocked off that it was taking too long to recover each time, and they were afraid they'd wipe it out completely, so they stopped, but I was ready to stop.'

He hung on tight, and she hung on back, remembering the time she would really, really rather forget.

'Was it horrendous?'

'Not horrendous,' she said honestly, 'but not good. I felt sick—not horrifically, but I had a sore mouth, and so I didn't really want to eat or drink, so not being hungry was probably a bonus. And I was tired—so, so tired. I slept most of the time. And of course I lost my hair, and every time it started to grow back again, I'd have to go back in and have another cycle and it would fall out again. I'd go in for the infusion, then home for forty-eight hours, then back in, in isolation, until my bone marrow had recovered, then I'd have a week or two at home before the next time. And they checked my bone marrow every time, and after the first cycle I was in remission, which is what they expect, but they have to go on to make sure they've got every last cell.'

'And have they?' he asked, and she could feel the tension building in him as he waited for her reply.

'Yes. I've been clear ever since, and they gave me the all-clear at five years, but they still test me every year— it's only a blood test, but they keep checking, and they'll do that for the rest of my life.'

'So it never goes away? The fear, the possibility of it returning?'

'Not really,' she said, thinking about it. 'I don't tend to dwell on it, but I suppose it's always there, and something like little Liam today brings it all right back.' She sighed. 'Poor Siobhan. I always thought my parents had a harder time of it than I did, especially my mother. It's really tough on a mother. I can't imagine what it must be like.' And she might never have the chance to find out…

'So what will happen to Liam? Will it be the same?'

'Pretty much, I expect. They'll do the bone-marrow aspiration tomorrow, and then if that confirms it's ALL, they'd do other tests to establish exactly which sort, because that determines which drugs they use to target it. And he'll have a series of treatments in a complex schedule over the next couple of years—it's a longer treatment for children, but the hospital staff will get them through it. They're fantastic. The nurses were brilliant to me.'

'Is that why you went into nursing? You said the other day you lived with nurses for a while—is that what you meant? In the hospital?' he asked, as if it had been puzzling him and he'd suddenly worked it out, and she nodded.

'Mmm. I hardly saw the doctors, really, but the nurses were there with me all the time, hands-on and much more involved with my daily care, and it just seemed—I don't know, more me, really. And it's nothing to do with being clever. Everybody thinks if you're clever enough you should be a doctor and not a nurse, but it's so different, and you have to be clever to be a decent nurse especially these days, it's got so complicated.'

'You're a brilliant nurse,' he said softly. 'Watching you today with Liam, knowing something was wrong but not knowing what, but just watching you with him, the way you got that blood from him when he was clearly terrified, but you just distracted him with the colour thing and he was too busy trying to prove you wrong to notice. And the way you dealt with the parents—you were fantastic. I'm not surprised she came to see you. I just wonder that they all don't.'

'Well, today was a little different. I'm not that nice to all of them.' She laughed, but he just smiled.

'I bet you are. It's not in your nature to be nasty to anyone. You were even nice to Gary Lovelace.'

'So were you.'

He gave a soft laugh. 'Let's face it, life was doing a pretty good job of having a go at him at that point, I didn't need to do it, too.'

'No.'

He held her quietly for a while, while she lay in his arms and let all the hurt seep away, and then he lowered his head and kissed her. 'Come to bed,' he murmured. 'I want to make love to you.'

It was dark in the bedroom, the only light the pale shimmer of the moon across the sea in the distance, and they lay snuggled together, her head on his shoulder— the right shoulder, the one that didn't hurt—and his left hand was trailing softly over her, his little finger stroking her skin, because he could still feel with that side of his hand and he wanted to feel her, needed to feel her, to make up for all the time they'd lost.

She was so soft, her skin like silk, and he turned his head and kissed her tenderly. 'I love you,' he said quietly. 'I'm so sorry I wasn't there for you. You do believe me when I say I would have been, don't you?'

Gemma nodded. 'I know, and I'm so sorry I shut you out, but I did it for you, Sam, you have to believe that. You had your whole life, your career ahead of you. You'd worked so hard for it, your life had already been hard enough. You'd had your mother depending on you, your sisters and your little brother—for the first time since your early teens you were going to be free to do what you wanted to do, so how could I ask you to take me on as well? I couldn't burden you, Sam. It wouldn't have been fair.'

He'd never thought of it like that, and never would. He would never have walked away, because it—she— would never have been a burden. 'It was my choice. It should have been my choice, Gemma.'

'I know. I can see that now, and I let you down,

because I didn't understand about love then. And if I'd told you, we could have been together, then you wouldn't have ended up in Africa, and you wouldn't have been blown up and so badly hurt.'

'I'm all right,' he said, but she shook her head, her eyes filling with tears.

'No, you're not. And you won't be, unlike me. Your leg's always sore, your shoulder hurts if you move it too far out of its comfortable range, your hand can't feel properly, so it makes your job and everything else difficult.'

'And does that worry you?'

'What?'

'Does it worry you? That I'm—disabled?'

'You're not disabled! Don't be ridiculous!'

'I am. You said it yourself. My ankle will never be right, my leg will never be right, I'll always have problems with my shoulder and permanent sensory deficit in my hand which affects what I can do career-wise—but would that stop you wanting to be with me? Would it make you walk away?'

She stared at him, horrified that he should even think it. 'Sam, of course not!'

'Then why did you think that I wouldn't want to be with you? You were *ill*, Gemz. You could have died, and you denied me the chance to support you, to be with you.'

'For you! And because of that, you went to Africa and got blown up.'

'Because of my own stupid fault! The accident was all my fault, I should have taken more care. I had a duty to look after myself, and I failed. It's not your fault that I was blown up, I should have paid attention. And I'm fine, I can live with it, but I can't live without you, and

I'm never letting you go again, whatever the future holds for us, because I can't live without you. I need you so much.'

He turned her into his arms and held her tight. 'Promise me you'll stay with me. I can't lose you again. I just can't…'

His voice broke, and he felt the tears he'd held back for so long forcing their way out past his defences, but it didn't matter because Gemma was holding him, and telling him it was all right, and she was crying, too, her tears hot on his shoulder, like healing rivers taking away the pain in his heart and filling it with love.

But she couldn't promise this. Not yet. Not before he knew it all. 'Sam, it may come back,' she warned tearfully, easing away so she could look at him.

His gaze didn't waver. 'I know.'

'I may die. I don't think so, and I'm clear, but there's no guarantee. And we may never have children— because of the chemo. And if that's important to you, you need to know that there's a real possibility I'm sterile. You need time to think about it, to work out what you want from a marriage, because I couldn't bear it if we got back together again now and then a few years down the line you changed your mind because we couldn't have children and you realised you wanted them more than me after all.'

'No. No way. Of course I want children with you— but that's the key. *With you.* And if you're clear, you're no more likely to get it back than I am. That's not going to change my mind, my darling. None of that is going to change how I feel about you. Children are optional. You're not. I need you—for as long as we've got together, I need you.'

'Oh, Sam.' She reached up and cradled his rough, stubbled face in her hand, feeling the rasp of it against her palm, real and solid. Her Sam. 'I need you, too,' she said unsteadily, tears falling again, 'and I've missed you so much.'

'No more,' he said, drawing her back against his chest so she could hear the steady, even beat of his heart beneath her ear. 'That's all finished now. We're starting again.'

For a moment they lay in silence, simply holding each other and treasuring the contact, then she said softly, 'Sam—can we do it properly this time? Have a church wedding?'

He gave a low chuckle. 'But we're still married, sweetheart. We don't need to get married again.'

She tipped her head back. 'I know, but—I'd just like to do it properly, with our families, and our friends.'

He smiled. 'In the church, I suppose?'

'Can we? Have a church blessing?'

'If that's what you'd like.'

'It is—on our wedding anniversary,' she said, getting into it, because not having a proper wedding with their loved ones there to hear their vows in public was one of the things she'd always regretted. 'Can we do that?'

'Sure. And maybe this time, when I say my vows, you'll trust me enough to believe me.'

'Oh, Sam, I'm so sorry,' she said, filled with endless regret.

'I know. So am I. But we're getting another chance, so let's use it wisely, and talk to each other. Promise?'

She smiled at him, her eyes shining. 'I promise.'

Their wedding anniversary dawned bright and clear, a glorious sunny day in early August.

They had breakfast together on the deck, watching the sun rise, and then she went to have a shower—and ended up with company, Sam smiling that sexy, lazy smile and lathering his hands and washing her, oh, so thoroughly all over, until she could hardly stand, and then carrying her back to bed and loving her until she came apart all over again, taking him with her.

And then she smiled at him and said, 'I've got something to give you.'

'A wedding anniversary present?' he said, puzzled when she went into the bathroom, but then she came out with a little white stick in her hand and gave it to him.

A pregnancy test stick. And it was positive.

He felt his eyes fill with tears, and he drew her into his arms and held her close, wondering why the hell being so happy should make him want to cry. But these last few months they'd shed a lot of tears together, for all the time they'd lost, and these—these were good tears.

'I can't wait to see you with our baby,' she said. 'You'll be such a good father, Sam. We're going to have a very lucky child.'

'With a mother like you, it can't fail,' he said, hugging her hard and hanging on.

And then they were late, and she had so much to do she began to panic, and she sent him away.

'Go! Go on, I want to do this properly, you'll have to wait for me in the church, and Lauren's going to come and help me dress, so scoot!'

He scooted, and went home to his mother's house and found her dithering in a panic because he wasn't dressed.

'You'll be late!' she scolded, back to herself now, and he hugged her and grinned at Jamie and ran an eye over his suit.

'Very smart. Never thought I'd see you in tails.'

'It's that woman you married, wanting to do everything properly,' he said with a grin. 'Go on, go and change or you'll be late.'

'You're beginning to sound like Mum,' he said drily, but he went and changed, because he couldn't get there quick enough.

They walked up, leaving a reluctant Digger behind, and went through the little lychgate to where Jeff Saunders, the new vicar who'd replaced Daniel Kenner, was waiting for them.

And the church was packed, to his surprise. Gemma's parents were waiting in the porch for him, and Gemma's mother came up to him and hugged him.

'I'm so sorry I sent you away. Please forgive me,' she said, and he felt his eyes fill and hugged her back hard.

'I know you were only doing what she asked,' he said. 'And it's behind us now.'

'She's coming!'

'Oh! Sam, in the church, you can't see her, it's unlucky!'

He hid a smile. Unlucky? He didn't think so. Not after the wedding anniversary present she'd given him that morning. He shook hands with Jeff Saunders, greeted their friends as he and Jamie walked down the aisle and took their places, and then the organist was playing and he turned his head and...

His breath caught in his throat.

She looked beautiful. More beautiful than he'd ever seen her, her face radiant, her eyes shining with love as she walked towards him on her father's arm, and as she drew level with him, he chucked convention out of the window and bent his head and kissed her.

'I love you, Mrs Cavendish,' he said softly, and she smiled.

'I love you, too. But we have an audience.'

He glanced over her shoulder and grinned. 'So we do. Perhaps we'd better get on with it.'

And he turned back to Jeff Saunders who was smiling indulgently, and nodded.

'Dearly beloved, we're gathered her today to bless the marriage of Gemma and Sam, and to give them an opportunity to make their vows again, in front of you, their family and friends, to cement their marriage and help them make a fresh start on this their journey together.'

And then Sam turned to her, took her hands and stared into her eyes.

'I, Samuel, take you, Gemma, to be my wife. To have and to hold, from this day forward, for better, for worse, for richer, for poorer, in sickness and in health, till death do us part. I promise to love and honour you, to trust you, to listen to you, to talk to you, to share my worries and my joys, and to be here for you, no matter what, as long we're both alive. Everything I have, everything I am, is yours. I love you.'

They'd written the words themselves, but as Gemma repeated them back to him, her voice caught.

'...in sickness...'

She faltered, and he held her hands as she lifted her eyes to his again, and went on, 'In sickness and in health, till death do us part. I promise to love and honour you, to trust you, to listen to you, to talk to you, to share my worries and my joys, and to be here for you, no matter what, as long we're both alive. Everything I have, everything I am, is yours. I love you.'

And with tears in their eyes, they went into each other's arms and held on tight, through all the readings, through the hymns, and through the final prayer, then, letting go, they joined their hands and turned back towards their family and friends, and took the first step of their onward journey.

Together...

1009/03a

Coming next month
COUNTRY MIDWIFE, CHRISTMAS BRIDE
by Abigail Gordon

Dr James Bartlett is captivated by new Willowmere midwife
Lizzie Carmichael. With the help of his adorable twins,
James wants to convince Lizzie that joining his little family
would be the perfect Christmas present for them all!

GREEK DOCTOR: ONE MAGICAL CHRISTMAS
by Meredith Webber

Neena Singh's unplanned pregnancy has left her wary of
men, so she firmly ignores her instant chemistry with Dr Mac
Stavrou! But Neena's unborn child is a Stavrou heir...and Mac
wants this beautiful Outback doctor as his Christmas bride!

HER BABY OUT OF THE BLUE
by Alison Roberts

When Dr Jane Walters donated her eggs for IVF, she never
anticipated gorgeous Dylan McKenzie walking into her life
holding *her* daughter! Miracle baby Sophie needs a family –
can Dylan and Jane make her Christmas wish come true?

A DOCTOR, A NURSE: A CHRISTMAS BABY
by Amy Andrews

This Christmas, paediatric nurse Maggie Green's dreams
of motherhood are about to come true! But how will top-
notch doc and confirmed bachelor Dr Nash Reece react
to Maggie's Christmas baby bombshell...?

On sale 6th November 2009

 **MEDICAL**™

Single titles coming next month

SPANISH DOCTOR, PREGNANT MIDWIFE
by Anne Fraser

When one amazing night with midwife Annie Thomas results in pregnancy, fiery Spaniard Dr Raphael Castillo is *determined* to be part of his baby's life! But Raphael must convince Annie that their adorable baby isn't the only one who has captured his heart…

EXPECTING A CHRISTMAS MIRACLE
by Laura Iding

Nurse Alyssa Locke didn't have a chance to tell Dr Jadon Reichart she was pregnant with twins before he walked away, but the discovery of this double miracle has turned this daddy-to-be's life upside-down! And if Alyssa accepts Jadon's Christmas proposal, this little family will have their festive happy ending!

On sale 6th November 2009

Available at WHSmith, Tesco, ASDA, Eason and all good bookshops.
For full Mills & Boon range including eBooks visit
www.millsandboon.co.uk

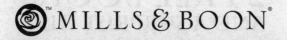

2 FREE BOOKS
AND A SURPRISE GIFT

We would like to take this opportunity to thank you for reading this Mills & Boon® book by offering you the chance to take TWO more specially selected books from the Medical™ series absolutely FREE! We're also making this offer to introduce you to the benefits of the Mills & Boon® Book Club™—

- **FREE home delivery**
- **FREE gifts and competitions**
- **FREE monthly Newsletter**
- **Exclusive Mills & Boon Book Club offers**
- **Books available before they're in the shops**

Accepting these FREE books and gift places you under no obligation to buy, you may cancel at any time, even after receiving your free books. Simply complete your details below and return the entire page to the address below. You don't even need a stamp!

YES Please send me 2 free Medical books and a surprise gift. I understand that unless you hear from me, I will receive 5 superb new stories every month including two 2-in-1 books priced at £4.99 each and a single book priced at £3.19, postage and packing free. I am under no obligation to purchase any books and may cancel my subscription at any time. The free books and gift will be mine to keep in any case.

Ms/Mrs/Miss/Mr _____ Initials _____

_____

Surname _____

Address _____

_____

_____ Postcode _____

Send this whole page to: Mills & Boon Book Club, Free Book Offer, FREEPOST NAT 10298, Richmond, TW9 1BR